THE F

THE FOGOU

by

Kenneth Ireland

LONDON : DENNIS DOBSON

First published in 1977 by
Dobson Books Ltd, 80 Kensington Church Street, London W8

Printed in Great Britain by
Bristol Typesetting Co, Ltd,
Barton Manor, St. Philips, Bristol

ISBN 0 234 72028 x

CONTENTS

CONTENTS

ONE

INITIATION

The boy with hair which tended towards a ginger colour sat on the front step of the cottage and watched a herd of cows come down the road and pass by him towards the church, followed by a boy on an old bicycle who was zig-zagging slowly behind the slowest-moving beast. He was about the same age as the boy on the step, but tanned from the waist up and wearing an old pair of blue jeans, with unpolished shoes on his feet. He rode in silence, and his sole job seemed to consist of persuading the cows at the back not to loiter. He glanced at the step but neither nodded nor smiled.

After the slow procession had passed, the boy on the step followed it with his eyes then got up and leaned on the gatepost until he saw it finally disappear to the right at the crossroads and into a wide farm gate, at which point the cyclist dismounted, closed the gate behind him and leaving his cycle walked after the cows and out of sight. After a few minutes the same boy reappeared, opened the gate, brought his bike out again, and closed the gate carefully and then rode slowly back along the road. When he reached the cottage, he stopped thoughtfully, with one foot on the ground.

'I thought Mrs Johnson wasn't letting her cottage this summer,' he said without preamble, 'what with her accident and all.' Then he paused, as if he had asked a question and was waiting for an answer.

'She's my great-aunt,' said the boy at the gatepost.

'Oh. So you're Colin. Her niece's son, are you?'

Colin paused before answering while he thought, then he

realized that this was not a city but a small village, and of course most of the inhabitants would know each other's business.

'Staying here long?' pursued the village boy.

'My mother thinks it will be about a month,' replied Colin. 'She's going to look after my great-aunt until she's able to get about. She's over at her house now—well, at her cottage. So we're living here in the meantime, because there's not enough room for us where my great-aunt lives.'

He recalled earlier that day, when the train had reached the end of its line at Penzance station, most of the passengers carrying their holiday suitcases. He and his mother had left the station and had stood irresolute at the crossroads outside, underneath the traffic lights, because that was where his great-aunt's letter had told them they would be met. Almost at once a local man aged about forty had moved over to them and asked if they were the ones to be taken to Geraint's Cove, and he had led them to the car park on the sea front and then had driven them the eight miles to the village.

'It was my uncle who brought you, then,' remarked the boy. 'He does run a kind of taxi service sometimes. Just for the village, of course. My dad, he reckons Mrs Johnson will be out and about before long. Even at her age, with a broken leg, it shouldn't take more than a month or two, he says.'

'How did she break it?' asked Colin with interest. No one had told him.

A slow smile crept across the cyclist's face, and Colin could not be sure whether he ought to count it callousness first to smile and then to grin when referring to such a painful experience for an elderly lady. 'Got walked on by a cow,' he said eventually. He eased himself forward until he was resting on the rusty black cross-bar with both feet flat on the roadway, then paddled himself to the edge of the road where the grass grew thickly as a tourist's car came up behind him and then passed by. 'You see, she's got this bike which she always rides, even just up the road to the shop, and the road was a bit muddy and she'd just gone through our cows on the way to milking. Well, her wheels slid in the mud, she fell off, and the cows didn't stop and one of them walked over her. She yelled fit to bust. Hard luck on her, though,' he added carefully, 'but you can't blame the old cow who did it, because she didn't know any better.'

Colin grinned as well, then asked if the farmer was the boy's father, but it turned out that he was another uncle.

'So you've not long been here?' The boy stated the obvious. 'I'm Fred. Perhaps if you're staying a month we'll get to know each other. How are you going to spend your time?'

Colin shrugged. He had no idea. He knew that Geraint's Cove was on the coast, but since he was alone and his mother looked like being occupied at his great-aunt's for much of the time, he had not yet felt like looking around to get his bearings. Added to this, train journeys, especially long ones, made him feel both tired and a little sick, and he was only within the last hour recovering.

The village seemed a dead-and-alive hole after living in a city, but the air smelled fresh, and there were gulls flying overhead all the time. The cove itself, wherever it actually was, seemed a popular place for holidaymakers, for even in the short time he had been out of doors plenty of cars had been heading along the road towards somewhere, and now it was becoming late afternoon just as many vehicles were returning in the direction of Penzance. He could imagine one of two things, either a sandy beach packed with trippers so there was hardly room to move about, or a pebbly stretch of shore and the cars all heading to and from another, prettier cove farther along the coast. He had visions of a petrol-smelling car-park in either event, with a man in a white coat collecting money. Anyway, it was better than Birmingham, he supposed, where it was all fumes and no seagulls.

'What is there?' he asked.

Fred looked at him incredulously. 'Of course, if you live in a town,' he said, 'you'd never find anything to do in one of those. Here there's lots to do. There's so much I don't find time to do it all, not everything I want to, anyway. We have a disco once a month, then there's the church youth club. There's fishing, and swimming, and fields and things. There's helping on the farm when my uncle's a bit short-handed or extra-busy. We haven't got a picture house, of course, but who wants one of those? And what do you do in a city, anyway?—I bet you sit watching television.'

'Don't you?'

'When I've nothing better. And sometimes when it turns a bit cool in the winter, or when it turns so wet you can't go out. Come on,' he said, 'and I'll show you the sights.'

He dumped the bike in the hedge and stood waiting. Colin saw that he was in fact about the same size as himself. He made some comment about locking up the cottage, but Fred poured scorn on the idea and said that nobody ever did that in the village. 'Anyway, what for? Who's going to take anything? Cars won't stop here, and nobody around here bothers about locks except at night in case there are strangers prowling.'

Fred set off up the road away from the farm, then since Colin was hardly out of his gate came back a few paces. 'Tell you what,' he said, 'if you can swim, I'll take you to a good place later on, when the trippers have gone. This road might seem quiet now, but give it another half an hour and cars will start pouring back the other way, going to where they're staying for their holidays sort of. You'll see. About tea-time, when everyone sets off back and at this time of the year it gets like—like—'

'Like Birmingham in the rush hour,' completed Colin, 'like New Street.'

'I wouldn't know about that,' replied the local boy seriously. 'You can keep your old towns. Except—' He glanced sidelong at Colin as he spoke—'except perhaps in a town it's better sometimes because you don't know everybody and you can't get forced into things.'

'Like what?' asked Colin, but the other did not answer,

possibly because they were now at the crossroads in the middle of the village.

There were cottages lining the roads, grey and white, and two shops side by side. A signpost with a wooden board indicated *To the Cove*. And beyond the small village lay the almost tree-less grassland of Cornwall, with fields marked out and a bare, dusty road. At the crossroads they stopped.

'Is this all there is?' asked Colin.

'I'll show you the cove,' said Fred, and led the way indicated by the sign.

The road led downwards, narrow and twisting, past some more houses standing in their own grounds, but most built of local stone nevertheless and only distinguished from their neighbours in the upper part of the village by being larger and grander—if only because of their separate gardens, and walls, and the occasional ornamental iron gate. Then the road took a final turn and ran along the edge of the sea, and the view was perfect.

The sea was blue, like the sea on a coloured picture post-card, and the light seemed somehow brighter and cleaner suddenly—purer almost. The low cliffs which rose round the little bay were a light brown colour, and the houses were of a light, clean, grey stone. Here were more shops, mainly selling pottery and art work and Cornish novelties, and one with ice cream and sweets. At the end of the road—and it was the end, because there was nothing beyond it—on the tiny harbour stood a public house, and as Colin had imagined a small car park with a man in a white coat standing guard, armed with a leather bag in which he kept the takings. In the harbour were some small boats, obviously locally-owned, mainly rowing dinghies but with also a larger, powered boat which might seat a dozen or so for trips out into the bay. A few brown nets were strung along the harbour wall to dry, and on the harbour itself stood a pile of lobster pots. A few local men in blue jerseys and sea-boots completed the scene, sitting around on the wall near the public house.

'So this is what it's all about!' exclaimed Colin, thinking how lucky his great-aunt had been, years ago, to marry a man who had lived here.

Fred looked at him curiously. 'Pretty isn't it?' he said, and led the way forward.

The cars were parked on asphalt but in front of them, nearer the water, was a tiny, sandy beach forming a kind of border to one side of the harbour. Sitting on an upturned rowing boat on one side of the beach was another boy who was perhaps a year or two older than Colin and Fred, dressed in old jeans.

'You're coming later, Fred?' he asked.

'Be all right if I bring him?' asked Fred in return. 'He's Mrs Johnson's relative, staying here with his mother while his great-aunt gets better.'

The boy on the boat inspected Colin with no great interest. 'Be all right, then,' he remarked. 'About the usual time, then.'

The conversation seemed to be over, and the boy on the rowing boat picked up a few stones and skimmed them carefully into the sea. Colin and Fred withdrew. Colin asked Fred where he had meant when he had asked if it was all right to take him. Fred said he meant when they went swimming. Colin examined the tiny beach.

'Aren't we coming here?'

'No. There's a much better place. Can you dive?' He seemed just a little anxious, and Colin wondered what he was letting himself in for, but he said that he could, and the other nodded his head as though satisfied. 'Better be getting back, then,' he said.

The whole thing seemed very curious, and Fred hardly spoke another word until they had climbed up the hill again to the crossroads in the village, where as Fred had predicted the traffic was now considerably heavier than it had been.

'You going along to your great-aunt's now?' asked Fred, and when Colin said he supposed he had better, because that was where he was expected for tea, Fred walked with him towards the church and round the corner to where Mrs Johnson's cottage stood, past the gate of the cottage where the two boys had first met. As they passed, Colin glanced at the cottage, but all seemed well.

'Now look,' said Fred, 'I'll meet you at the crossroads about half-six. Bring your bathers and a towel, and then I'll show you where we go. I can take you, because we know Mrs Johnson. Because you're a relation of hers, that almost makes you belong here, so that's all right.'

Then he departed, and Colin opened the door of the cottage where his mother was expecting him after his afternoon's rest, and went inside. It surprised him to find the old lady downstairs, sitting in a chair with a pair of wooden crutches lying on the carpet beside her.

'Well, give me a kiss, then,' she commanded, and he did. She was much older than he had expected, not having seen her since he was very small. 'Have you recovered now?' she asked rather fiercely. 'Long journeys don't suit me, either, so perhaps it runs in the family. You've certainly grown since I saw you last.' She examined him critically but did not appear to be dissatisfied.

His mother came from the kitchen carrying plates, which she laid on the table, and she asked if he had just come from the cottage.

'I've been down to the harbour,' he said, 'and a local boy's asked me if I could go swimming after tea.'

Before his mother could make any comment, Great-Aunt Daphne asked sharply which local boy, so Colin told her what he knew of him.

'Ah, that'll be Fred Pope,' said the great-aunt, nodding her head. 'He's all right.'

'Where will you go swimming?' asked his mother.

'There's a cove just over the hill,' said his great-aunt. 'Motorists drive down to the harbour and think that's it, if they haven't visited here before, but if they have any sense they go out through the village on the main road and then take the next turn left. There's a sign saying *Cove* there as well, but it's a different cove. That's the real Geraint's Cove. Where everybody thinks is Geraint's Cove is really Geraint's Harbour. Local boys swim there when the tourists have gone home in the evenings. Not that you'll go along the road to it,' she added to Colin, 'because no doubt Fred will take you along the cliff path.'

Colin's mother was a little anxious at hearing that, and was worried that it might not be safe. A widow since Colin had been eight, she was naturally more than usually protective, but her aunt pooh-poohed the thought at once.

'Quite safe,' she said firmly. 'They all use it, and we haven't lost one yet. Now wash your hands and help your mother get the tea ready.' And as he went into the kitchen to find the soap and the sink he heard her remark that there was more danger crossing the road in a town than walking along the cliff path. He also heard her make some remark which he did not quite catch that the Popes were all right, but she couldn't say as much about one or two of the other boys.

Even if he had not known, he would have guessed that Great-Aunt Daphne was a retired schoolmistress who used to stand no nonsense from her charges in the village school. When he returned he asked if he had done right in not locking up the cottage before he had left it.

'You haven't left it open?' said his mother, aghast.

His great-aunt smiled and seemed not at all as frosty as she had first appeared. 'That'll be Fred Pope put you up to it,' she said. 'It's quite safe. We don't lock doors round here, unless we go away. It seems to me that he's adopted you into the village, telling you our little secrets. Very like his father he is, taking to some people and detesting others on sight. And both of them idle when there's something they'd rather do than the work that they should.' Colin had a suspicion that this indicated that his great-aunt had taught both Fred and his father, and that she was talking about school, but he could not be certain.

'Are you going to sit at the table?' his mother asked his great-aunt.

'I expected to see you in bed,' said Colin as Great-Aunt Daphne struggled to her feet and hobbled across the little room.

'Not the modern way, I'm told. "Walk about," they said, "don't just lie in bed." So I do. But I shan't be going upstairs for a little while.' She indicated a curtain across one end of the room. 'I sleep in there.'

She plonked herself down into a chair at the table and Colin decided that he quite liked his dragon of a great-aunt, especially when after tea was over she said that he had to do the washing-up and give his mother a rest, and added with a smile that the sooner he got the job done the sooner he would be able to get back to the cottage, find his swimming things and be off to enjoy himself. 'You can't expect your mother to keep following you around and holding your hand. I know she's come here to look after me, but it's got to be a change for her as well after living all that time in a dirty town. So if you've got your friends, you do your share of the jobs around the house and then enjoy yourself, and that'll give your mother time to enjoy herself without having to worry about you. We'll work out what your share is tomorrow.'

Then while his mother and her aunt talked happily in the one other room downstairs, he did the washing of the dishes in the kitchen, and afterwards ran off to collect his towel and his trunks, and then on to the crossroads to meet Fred.

Fred was already waiting when he arrived, and smiled a welcome. He had his shirt on this time, and looked as if his mother had made him have a wash, and underneath his arm he carried a clean towel rolled up surprisingly neatly. They set off down the road which led to the harbour, and then suddenly Fred led him through a gap in the hedge and along a path which took them towards the cliffs in the near distance.

The cliffs were higher than Colin had thought, and the

pathway wound along the top of them for perhaps half a mile and then began a sharp descent. It was warm, but not as warm as it had been earlier in the afternoon, and the sun still shone brightly but lower in the sky as a spectacular cove appeared in view, with the path now almost forming steps as it turned into rock. The last twist in the path actually were steps, concrete ones, to allow access over its last few yards to a wide, white beach of soft sand. Down here, the heat continued to be emitted from the dark cliffs of serpentine rock and the warm sand of this sun trap—far better, as his great-aunt had said, than bathing from the little beach in the harbour would have been. The sand was soft enough to make walking difficult until they had both taken off their plimsolls and socks and carried on in bare feet.

There were still some holidaymakers on the beach, but those few were all beginning to pack their belongings, shaking blankets and towels and generally making an exodus towards the concrete steps. The café which stood on a little rocky plateau above the beach was already closed, and the little wooden tables outside it had been wiped clean.

'Where are the others, then?' wondered Colin.

'Just round here,' said Fred.

About five or six boys were scattered around the rocks and the entrances of a number of tall, shallow caves or in the sea.

'Coming in?' asked Fred.

'You bet,' said Colin, and after they had changed found that his body looked unhealthily white compared with the tanned torsos of everyone else present. Still, he thought, they live here all the year round, and he reckoned that a week or two would soon prevent his looking like a visitor.

'Who've you brought?' asked a dark-haired boy of about their age who didn't pause as he sped like a fish towards them and the shore when they were still only waist-high in the water.

'Colin. He's staying a month,' replied Fred. 'Mrs Johnson's relation,' he added in further explanation.

'That's all right, then,' said the youth. 'Watcha, Ginger.'

Colin waved vaguely as he and his new friend plunged in.

'That rock,' announced Fred, swimming towards it, so of course Colin had to follow. He found to his delight that he was overtaking Fred and beat him to it, then helped him out to sit alongside. They surveyed the scene. The number of boys had grown until now there were perhaps nine or ten on the beach or in the sea.

'Everyone seems,' he said calmly, 'to be suspicious of strangers. There was that one down at the harbour, the one you had to ask if I could come, then that one who spoke to us just now.'

He had not asked a question, but managed to imply that it was one.

'We don't have many strangers down here,' said Fred equally calmly and matter-of-fact. 'We get lots of those on holiday, like, but we don't pay much attention to them, and they don't hang about with us because we don't let them. After a week they've gone anyway, and they always tag around with their parents. But you're here for a long time, and you're with Mrs Johnson.'

'Does that make a difference?'

'My dad and my uncles still get told off by her, they say, when she feels like it, so it's got to make a difference. The village got quite an upset when she got walked on by that cow. Everyone was round asking, "Are you all right, Mrs Johnson? What shall we do, Mrs Johnson? And there she lay on the ground giving them orders and making them run around.'

'She seems very old. Did she teach them?' Colin was interested to know.

Fred looked at him and smiled. 'And me, till I left the primary school. She was a tartar. Kept saying my uncles and my father were just as idle, she did.'

Colin smiled too, then they were off the rock and swimming back to the sands. By now there were—he counted—eleven boys altogether on the beach, including himself, and the rest were heading towards the far end, where there seemed to be some kind of ampitheatre formed by high, black rocks. The outer edge of the rocks left a narrow opening to the sea, which was now running in slowly to fill a natural bathing pool. It was growing a little darker, and just slightly cooler, and the others were draping themselves on the rocks all round except at the highest point, where there was a narrow ledge about three feet from the top. There was a feeling of expectancy and chattering was coming to an end and a silence began to wash over everything, like the sea coming into the pool below.

'What's everyone waiting for?' he asked.

'You'll see.'

Then one boy, who had been sitting on the rocks near the lowest point, dropped into the water and began to swim around, slowly, and at length climbed out again on to a table of rock which just showed above the surface now. 'It's okay,' he announced in a loud voice to everyone. 'It's deep enough.'

At this, a taller boy, the one whom Colin had previously seen seated on an upturned boat in the harbour, and who had been lounging near the highest point, got to his feet and climbed to the pinnacle, then cautiously lowered himself until he was standing on the narrow ledge. He seemed a considerable distance above the water. There was complete silence now, with everyone watching intently. The boy glanced carefully around the assembly, leaning back slightly with his hands grasping the rock behind him, then he stood erect, stretched out his arms and held himself poised.

Then he dived straight down. A sort of sigh passed round the group as he rose to the surface and swam strongly to the side. Colin was somewhat nervous. Was this what Fred had been referring to when he had asked him if he could dive? And did it mean that everyone had to have a go? He peered up at the ledge, then down towards the water. From where he was, it looked very high, but he could see that while it might also appear to be high to one standing on the ledge, in fact there was an element of optical illusion about it. It was not as high as imagination could make it appear. He doubted that it was as far from the water as the diving board in the swimming baths. The only problem was not to fall off the ledge before one was ready, and to avoid hitting one's head on that flat chunk of rock.

Another older youth ascended to the pinnacle and lowered himself to the ledge in a second bout of silence, and when he at last dived, after looking as if he were about to change his mind, Colin noticed that in fact he avoided the chunk of rock by at least eight feet. Colin decided that it was not as difficult as it looked. It just needed a lot of nerve to do it the first time, in case one looked a fool, as might happen if one made a mess of getting on to that ledge, and a little care in choosing the right point to enter the water.

The first youth had sat and watched the second one impassively, from a point high up the rocks, and he was equally impassive when another volunteer took his place. Colin observed that only the older boys were making any effort to perform the dive, and the younger ones remained near the bottom end of the pool. It was now a shade darker still, and noticeably cooler possibly because of a sea-breeze which had begun to blow gently. The whole place had become a little eerie.

'Going to have a go, Ginger?' called the dark-haired one whom he had encountered in the sea.

Everyhead turned towards Colin and Fred.

'Let's see you first,' said Colin loudly.

Without a word, the dark-haired boy moved up the rocks like a pale monkey, slithered down to the ledge, and dived. When he had climbed out, he sat in the same place as before. It was almost as if there was a kind of seating order in some sort of secret society meeting.

'If you want to come here again, let's see you do it now, Ginger,' called the boy who had dived first, who seemed to be the acknowledged leader of whatever was taking place.

Now that Colin inspected him, even across the distance, more carefully, he was not just a year or so older than Fred and himself, but was at least seventeen or so. Every head turned again towards Colin expectantly, and Colin suddenly realized where he had encountered a similar gathering. It had been when he had seen apes on the rocks in the enclosure at the zoo. They too had sat, apparently doing nothing but waiting for something to happen.

He rose lazily but with a slight fear inside him, more from the likelihood of making a fool of himself than from anything else, and scrambled up the rocks to the top. At one point he slipped, and he heard a faint jeer from somewhere, but he recovered his footing and continued to the pinnacle as if nothing had happened and finally looked down from the top.

The pool was below him, green not blue and absolutely still on its surface, except at the side where the tide entered slowly. All the heads of the boys were turned towards him, and there was complete silence. The ledge appeared too far down and too narrow to reach in safety, but having attained that position he could not back out now, so he sat on the rock which was now cold and rough to the backs of his thighs and lowered his feet over the edge and as slowly as he dared dropped down. Where his feet landed, it felt as smooth as concrete, and not at all slippery, so he leaned backwards slightly to retain his balance and glanced down with care. From up there, the flat rock seemed to be too much in the way, and dangerous, but he knew that if he thought first he was unlikely to come to harm.

He stood upright, took a breath and raised his arms in front of him as he had been taught at school, then plunged, arms forward, legs together and straight so they would not tilt over to cause an undignified splash as he entered the water. As soon as his hands were under he tilted them upwards slightly to bring himself almost at once back to the surface, and then swam gently and with a superior feeling inside of him to the table rock. He also felt a little angry at having been made to perform in this way without warning in front of a critical audience.

'For an encore,' he called insolently towards the dark, older figure at the top of the rocks, 'I shall now show you how to do a breast-stroke to the edge of the pool.' And he did, as if giving a demonstration, climbed out, swept his hair back to help remove some of the water from it, and returned to his seat alongside Fred Pope.

'You'll do, Ginger,' said the leader, seemingly not at all put out.

Nobody else seemed willing to dive any more that evening, and in the fading light some boys drifted off the rocks to get changed, others dived in and swam around as they might in a public swimming bath, and the leader and the dark-haired youth scrambled down towards Colin and Fred, who were moving off towards where they had left their clothes in order to dry and change.

'You'll do,' said the leader again, when he had come closer. 'Now this is a sort of society, see? We come here on a lot of evenings in the summer. You can join us if you like, but the first thing you've got to learn is to keep your mouth shut.'

'Yeah,' said the dark-haired boy. 'It's a sort of secret society.'

'What's so secret?' asked Colin. 'Great-Aunt Daphne knows you come here.'

'She knows most things around here,' remarked the leader, nodding, 'but she don't know everything. We don't have many secrets, really, but it makes it more interesting. Doesn't it?' he said suddenly to Fred.

Fred looked startled, as if he was afraid of something.

'So what I say goes,' observed the leader, 'and no matter what, nobody else is ever told. Get it? And once you're in, you're in. No backing out.'

'Yeah,' said the dark-haired boy. 'Once you're in, no back-out, and no telling tales.'

It sounded interesting, even if childish. Colin wondered

what it was that they actually did, but if diving from the ledge was the worst part of it—and he assumed that had been some sort of initiation test to try him out—then he would be happy enough to pass some time with them.

'All right,' he said.

'We'll see.' All at once Colin was in agony as the leader reached out with both hands and gave him a severe Chinese burn on his left wrist, by seizing a section of skin in each hand and twisting fiercely in opposite directions. Colin cried out, then looked down to where a reddening was appearing on the flesh. There was certainly something unpleasant about this youth who claimed to be the leader of the boys of the village.

'Going to tell your mother?' asked the leader.

Colin looked him in the face. 'No,' he said.

The leader's face became a smile. 'Well done,' he said. 'Then now you're one of us.' He turned away. 'All right, you lot. See you in two nights' time,' he called, then walked round the side of the rocks and disappeared somewhere.

Colin and Fred carried on drying themselves, then dressed in silence, and eventually set off back towards the village by themselves.

'Who is he?' Colin asked at length.

'Derek. He lives at the café on the beach.' He spoke a little apologetically, as if he had led Colin into something which Colin might regret. 'He's all right, as long as you don't cross him.'

'But why does everyone follow him?'

Fred shrugged, and didn't answer. They were at the village crossroads, and it was nearly dark.

'I'm going home. See you.'

While Fred set off in one direction, Colin walked off in the other. He had seen there were no lights in the cottage where he and his mother were staying, so he carried straight on towards Great-Aunt Daphne's, where his mother no doubt would still be waiting.

TWO

THE BOAT IN THE CAVE

Colin's bedroom was the one on the front of the cottage, with its window overlooking the road, while his mother slept at the back. She seemed to be enjoying her stay thoroughly so far, which surprised him a little, because he could not see that looking after an old woman was any sort of holiday at all. He had to assume that it was the change of surroundings which she appreciated, and after all, he reasoned, she was with him in their own home all the year round, so it was not unnatural that she would like a complete change of scenery, including not seeing as much of him as she usually did. Added to that, his great-aunt who seemed to know everyone and everything in the district was not discouraging about his going around with Fred Pope, and his mother was clearly quite agreeable. What was it the old lady had said?—'Do your share of the chores about the house, then go off and enjoy yourself.' All right, then, that's what he would do.

When he drew back the curtains and looked out, it was as sunny and warm as it had been the previous day. The hot summer was going to continue for a long time yet. He went down to wash, and found a note on the kitchen table: 'Come to Aunt Daphne's for breakfast.'

So as a regular inhabitant of the village, and not just a holidaymaker, after a quick wash he closed the door but did not lock it and set off towards the other cottage. His great-aunt was reading the morning paper when he arrived, through large, steel-rimmed glasses. 'Good morning, Colin,' she said briskly. 'Let me see behind your ears.' She turned his hair back critically. 'That's all right then, you've washed. Now here's how we're going to work things out. Get your breakfast while I'm telling you.'

He helped himself to cornflakes and sat at the table. He rather liked this old lady's no-nonsense approach, straight to the point and little room for argument. With only himself and his mother at home, he was often able to wheedle out of her what he wanted, even if occasionally he won only because his mother with a flash of annoyance would end by telling him he could do what he liked for all she could care. He had a shrewd idea that none of that would work here.

'You will wash up after breakfast and after tea, and if your mother and I are in a hurry to go out, after dinner as well. If we're not going out early in an afternoon, you will be let off washing up midday.'

'Going out?' he asked in surprise.

'You don't think I'm going to be stuck in here all day and every day, do you? Now your mother is here, of course I can go out if I want to, because there will be somebody to help me. Besides, I intend that your mother shall go on excursions, not be tied to this village and an old woman all the time. Now. It's your job to keep the cottage in order. You will keep it neat and tidy, so that your mother doesn't have two houses to bother about. That means dusting and cleaning and making the beds. Apart from that, as long as you behave yourself you can join in with whatever the village boys are doing. Does that seem fair?'

Colin said through a mouthful of cornflakes that he supposed it was quite all right. 'Where's Mum?' he asked.

'Gone to the shop. You got up so late, half the day's gone, so when you've had your breakfast you can start on the washing-up. And chew your food, don't gulp it. Then this afternoon your mother's taking me to the hospital, so you can either come with us or stay in the village. I expect you'll want to go to the beach, won't you?'

24

Great-Aunt Daphne supposed correctly. Colin did not fancy a sunny afternoon surrounded by a smell of antiseptic, and said as much, bluntly, as his great-aunt might have done. She beamed in delight. 'Before you actually arrived,' she said, 'I wasn't sure whether I'd be seeing one of those city hooligan types we hear so much about—and see around here occasionally—although I thought Mary's boy would hardly turn out like that—or whether you'd be a mother's boy who hadn't a single thought of his own. I'm pleased that I was wrong on both counts.

'Well, when you've done eating, you know what you're to do.'

While he was replacing the dried dishes in the dresser he was struck with a thought.

'Great-Aunt,' he began, but was cut short at once.

'I don't like that,' she said. 'It makes me feel old, so you had better call me Aunt Daphne.'

'Well then, Aunt Daphne, who is Derek, who lives in the café by the cove?'

Aunt Daphne screwed up her mouth a little in distaste. 'His father lived in this village, then moved out to somewhere or other to make his fortune. He didn't make his fortune, so came back again and took over the café. They've been back for about three years. Derek Trewan tries to be the leader of the gang—I suppose you came across him yesterday. He's a bit shiftless, like most of his breed. His mother ran off to London or somewhere, years ago.' She dismissed the entire family with a sniff. 'Just don't start taking to his ways, and you should be all right. Oh, that reminds me, Fred won't be about for most of the day, so there'll be no point in looking for him. He's had to go with his father somewhere.'

Then his mother returned with the provisions, armed with a large, laden wicker shopping basket, and greeted him cheerily. He had not seen her look so happy for a long time, as if whatever cares she had had were now completely dispersed in the fresh air and sunshine. She also looked much younger. She seemed to fit the farming-fishing community, that was it, and he wished that he could bring about some method of keeping her and himself in that village rather than return to the Midlands, and rather that she should have to spend every day as a secretary in some office in the city centre. He knew the problem, though. What work could she find to do out here—or himself, for that matter, when he had grown up and left school—for jobs were not so plentiful, he knew, in Cornwall as in his own industrial district? He had read about it in the newspapers, that even farm workers were looking for jobs, and that the tourist trade, even, was depressed.

So he dismissed the idea from his mind and decided to do a week's cleaning in a morning, and returning to the cottage dusted, swept, cleaned, polished, washed windows, shook rugs —everything he could think of, like an over-enthusiastic girl he thought and hoped none of the village boys should pass by and see him or he might have something to live down. When he had finished he inspected every room and decided that apart from bed-making he had the place clean enough to last for at least a week, so that was his main job finished for the time being.

In the afternoon, when he *had* done the dishes, because an ambulance called early to collect his great-aunt to take her to the hospital and his mother had gone with her, he collected his bathers and wandered off to the sandy cove by himself. At this time of day the cove was swarming with visitors, so he laid his cast-off clothes by an outcrop of rock, near to where an elderly couple looked as if they intended to spend the afternoon sun-bathing on huge towels, and explored.

The cove was at the end of a little peninsula. From the foot of the concrete steps which he and Fred had used the previous evening stretched an expanse of beach winding in and out of the rocks. Beyond where he thought this beach had ended when last he had visited, however, because the tide was now fairly well out was exposed a second beach. On the opposite side of the peninsula, a matter of a hundred yards or so, was joined yet a third beach, the one where he and Fred had gone to join the others, and at the end lay the pool and the ampitheatre. He had noticed the tall caves before, but he had not realized just how many of them existed. It seemed that every few yards a new cave appeared, some just little impressions in the rock, others enormous cavities which were so extended to the rear that they were almost in darkness.

He had a quick swim in the sea, out to the rock again, then he tried the other beaches in turn. He found that the water temperature differed according to which side of the cove he was swimming, and at last settled for the beach on which he had left his clothes. He glanced first to ensure they were still there, then entered the water where the formation of the land caused a wave to hit first the farther of the two beaches, then the beach where he was standing, then as the water drew back to be assaulted by a second wave as it rushed in. The effect was that an enormous ridge of water would rise up some yards from the shore. Time and again he dived through the watery mountain until he was thoroughly refreshed and pretty well exhausted, then after a lazy swim around he stepped on to the sand again.

The place was fantastic. It was not only pretty; he was not much concerned with that, but the fact that the cove was like something out of a dream, a complete fantasy if he had not seen it for himself. It possessed everything—rocks to climb, white sand to lie on while the sun dried most of you, caves to explore, and a warm sea in which to enjoy yourself, and a café for ice cream or something to eat and drink. At the thought of the café he frowned a little. It stood on its rocky plateau above the first of the three beaches, reached by some rough steps cut into the serpentine rock, and had a queue of people outside. It obviously did a good trade.

He had just thought of exploring the caves properly, since there was nothing else to do, when he noticed a man sifting through the fine sand with his fingers. The man was wearing a tee-shirt and flared jeans and sandals, as if he were trying to look a little younger than he really was, and Colin saw a tiny bald patch on the crown of his head as he bent down. It was hardly the place for shells, so Colin watched for a moment out of curiosity, and as he did so his shadow fell across. The man looked up, smiled, and carried on feeling his way through the sand.

'I don't think you'll find any shells,' remarked Colin helpfully, in his role of a local inhabitant.

'It's not shells, it's a blessed gold ring. I just dropped the thing and the sand's so soft I'm not sure where it might be.'

Colin dropped down on his knees and after watching solemnly for a few seconds began to assist, running his fingers carefully through the surface of the beach. Neither of them found the missing ring, and at last the man stood up and looked at him. 'I don't think we're doing it systematically,' he said. 'Look, let's mark the area out in squares. I know it's down here somewhere.' He drew lines on the sand roughly with his forefinger, to mark out an area of about six feet square. 'Now, if you could start at that end and work your way towards the centre, I'll begin at this side and work my way towards you. One square at a time, mind.'

Facing each other, they began. Colin started at one edge, feeling through the sand and passing it slowly out behind him through his legs, like a dog digging in slow motion, then he moved to the next square alongside it, and continued until the first row of squares had been searched thoroughly. Finally—

'Here it is!' exclaimed Colin, holding up a thick, plain gold ring. It looked rather similar to the one his mother always wore.

'Well done; you're a smart boy,' responded the man, rising and taking it from him. 'Went on a weight-watching course once,' he explained, 'and I've been thinking for a year that I ought to have it made smaller. It drops off too easily, see?'

'You don't want to lose it,' said Colin automatically, thinking more of getting to the caves.

'You on holiday here, then?' asked the stranger.

'Sort of,' said Colin, 'But I've got a relative in the village and we're staying for some time. So I'm sort of—half a resident.'

'A temporary resident,' corrected the man, 'sounds more like it. I'm something of the same.'

'I'll have to go now,' said Colin. 'Perhaps see you around.' And he skipped off to investigate more interesting matters.

Most of the caves, however, were not especially interesting. For one thing, many of them were very similar, even the deeper ones. They didn't go anywhere. Many of them, too, were occupied by visitors or their clothing, and what visitors there were regarded him somewhat suspiciously when he began to wander around too closely. He wondered what enjoyment they could find sitting in a cool, shady cave doing nothing in particular when they could be better engaged out in the sun or the sea, acquiring a decent tan. His own body still proclaimed that he was new to the area, like most of theirs.

One of the caves, however, promised much better, for this was empty of people and from its far end led a dark, narrow passageway going off to the left with no light shining through. He stepped gingerly down the passage, gingerly because he had noticed that several of the tourists had brought their pet dogs with them, when the passage took a sharp turn to the right and there in front of him was a second cave opening out on to the beach nearest to the diving pool.

The sand in this cave was quite dry, indicating that it was above the level of the tide. Under an old tarpaulin sheet lay what appeared to be a boat, so he lifted one corner and peered inside. It was a boat. There was no one about, so he threw the tarpaulin back further until half the width of the boat was uncovered. It was a rowing boat, and the oars were laid neatly along the bottom. For a rowing boat it was fairly large, bigger than those he had seen bobbing about in the harbour, and at the stern was a bracket of a kind he had seen before, which he knew was designed to carry an outboard motor.

He covered the boat up again and walked out on to the beach. This section was entirely in shade, and so it was empty of people. When he turned back to the cave he saw a figure inside, standing by the boat and watching him.

'Hi, Ginger,' the figure called.

'Hello, Derek,' he said, and turned back. 'Whose is the boat?'

'My father's.'

'I thought you'd be busy in the café this afternoon,' remarked Colin pleasantly.

'Ah, well, I was, but the girl's turned up now so I can come out for half an hour.'

'Where do you go in it?'

'The boat?' Derek paused for a moment as if thinking of a suitable answer. 'Just row around every now and then. Do you want to come out in her?'

Colin needed no second urging, and discovered that it was a simple job to drag the dinghy across the sand. When they reached the water's edge and the boat was just beginning to float with its stern still firmly on the beach, Derek climbed in and asked Colin to push them further out before coming on board himself. 'You can get wet and it won't matter,' he said, which seemed a fair statement since he was fully clothed.

While Colin pushed the boat clear, the other took out the oars and fitted them into the rowlocks. Then they rowed around aimlessly for a while, until they were clear of the tiny headland and almost out at sea. There Derek laid down the oars for a moment, extracted a packet of cigarettes from the top pocket of his open lumber jacket and offered Colin one. The latter shook his head, so Derek struck a match, shielding the flame in his hands and lit one for himself before throwing the match into the sea.

'Want a row?' he asked, leaning back.

'Where shall we go?' asked Colin, leaving his seat with eagerness and taking the oars.

'Oh, around. Anywhere. Don't lose the oars overboard, or you'll have to get out and swim after them, since you're dressed for it.'

Colin was glad of the exercise, because now they were away from the shore the breeze made him feel chilly since he was wearing almost nothing. Derek watched him critically, saying nothing, but was clearly noting how well Colin could handle a boat. Then he threw the blackened end of the cigarette away and told Colin to turn the boat round and row back to the cave. 'Can't stay out too long,' he said in explanation. 'Got to get back to the customers.'

It was a harder pull to return the boat to the cave, and once there they swung it round so that its bows were pointing towards the sea again.

'Thanks for the ride,' said Colin.

'Come and have an ice cream,' said Derek, and in silence they felt their way through the passage, walked out of the cave at the other end and set off to the café above the beach, where Colin was solemnly handed an ice cream at the front of the queue.

'Some cups in there,' said a craggy-faced man behind the counter, nodding towards an inner door which presumably led into a kitchen. This must have been the youth's father. Colin did not like the look of him. Derek nodded vaguely at Colin and went into the kitchen.

'I like your boat,' said Colin to make conversation.

The man behind the counter finished handing change to a woman customer. 'What boat?' he said.

'The one down on the beach,' said Colin in surprise.

'Yes, please?' the man asked the next in line, and while he was serving two cups of tea added: 'I know nothing about a boat. I know there's one down there, but it's nothing to do with me.'

'Aren't you Mr Trewan?' asked Colin.

'Yep. But I know nothing about a boat. Now if you've got all you want, could you go outside? You're in the way of the customers.'

Colin, deciding that he liked the man even less, left, climbed down to where he had left his clothes, and since he was dry rubbed his feet to remove the last particles of sand, put on his shoes and carried his clothes under his arm until he reached the cottage. He thought with a wry smile that you couldn't walk around Birmingham dressed only in swim trunks and shoes without everyone taking the mickey out of you, but here nobody minded in the least.

Nevertheless, there was something distinctly odd about this village. There was something queer about the whole business, he decided. And who was lying—Derek or his father, because one of them had to be?

Fred was back in time to take the cows for milking, and the procession passed along the road shortly after Colin had returned to the cottage.

'Going to the cove tonight?' shouted Colin.

'Can't tonight,' replied the other, 'because it's choir practice.'

This was another surprise.

'Choir practice?' repeated Colin, looking at Fred in disbelief.

'Oh yes. We're all in the choir.'

'Even Derek?'

'Him as well, though sometimes he can't turn up.'

Since the village was going to be dead for the evening, therefore, after he had washed the tea things he listened to Aunt Daphne's concise opinion of doctors and nurses in general and to his mother's amused account of how Aunt Daphne had grown more and more frustrated as she discovered that she could not have her own way entirely at the hospital in Penzance—in which amusement the great-aunt had gradually joined in. Then he wandered off to the cove again, because he had nothing else to do. He could hardly offer to join the choir, because without a great effort he seldom managed to hit two consecutive notes correctly. Anyway, he didn't intend to offer his services.

Down at the cove, the tide was well in, and the café was closed. He amused himself by using rocks as stepping stones to pass over areas where the sea had covered.

On reaching the second cave he suddenly noticed that the boat had vanished, including the tarpaulin, and marks on the sand indicated where the boat had been dragged down to the water. He walked swiftly across to see if he could find it anyway. It was visible on the water, with Derek rowing vigorously sea-ward, and from the distance from the shore he had not long before set off.

The boat passed round the headland and disappeared from view. Colin wondered where Derek could be going, for it was growing dusk and it seemed a strange time for a row.

There were a few minutes of silence apart from the piping of gulls, then from the distance he could hear the engine of a boat, a steady chugging of a diesel-engined craft, and into sight appeared what seemed to be a boat which he had observed before—the trippers' boat from the harbour. Towing behind it, however, was now an empty rowing dinghy, and on the boat itself he could see quite clearly the figures of Derek Trewan and two men.

Then the boat set out towards the open sea and slowly disappeared from sight.

THREE

SIMON'S DIVE

At the amphitheatre in the rocks it was quiet. Out at sea, the sun after a day's expenditure of energy was sidling exhausted and yellow into the horizon, surrounding by a redness in the sky which boded well for the following day. Large shadows were being cast and while those boys near the top of the circle were illuminated in gold, or those with their backs to the dying sun were black, sinister shapes against the sky, the rest sitting clear of the sun's rays were almost in darkness. The water in the pool looked uninviting and cold. Colin noticed that despite the later time of the meeting the tide was only half-in, and the top of the table rock was standing several inches out of the water.

He was not sure why it was so quiet. The boys spoke in whispers to each other, if they talked at all, and this seemed very odd, as if they were gathered in the hush of a cathedral. There was a kind of expectancy. Another thought which crossed his mind was to wonder why no girls ever appeared at these meetings. There could, of course, be a number of reasons. An obvious one was that the boys changed on the beach, and perhaps did not relish the idea of girls being around at the time, although he would have thought that with all the caves down at the cove there would have been no problem at all. Another possibility was that this was deliberately a boys' club, and girls were just not welcome. Perhaps these boys had enough of seeing girls in the village and wanted to get away from them—but again, now he came to think of it, he had seen very few girls who actually lived in the village anyway. Just a plain lack of talent, he thought. Or it could be just one of those things which happened in some villages.

Then again, of course if what Fred had said was true, these boys were in the church choir. There was a church youth club, and presumably that was mixed, so this might be the opportunity to have their own boys' club and run it all by themselves, so to speak.

Derek appeared near the top of the rock, and the vague whisperings ceased altogether.

'What's going to happen tonight?' he muttered to Fred.

Fred looked worried, and shook his head not as if he did not know but as if he was not going to say. In a way, it seemed so silly, sitting round a half-full pool of cool water, in bathing gear, when an evening breeze was beginning to spring up from the sea-ward side of the beach. The dark-haired boy had also appeared near the top of the rocks, to squat near Derek. From over on the right among the rocks there seemed to be a little struggle breaking out, caused by a slightly younger boy, but it soon subsided.

Derek clambered to the pinnacle, the lowered himself to the ledge and looked down at the water as if measuring. Then he dived, suddenly, and as he surfaced a sound like a gasp ran round the assembled group of a dozen or so who were there. Derek swam to the edge of the water and several hands helped him out and he climbed to the top again. He stood, dripping water.

'We all know the rules,' he announced quietly enough but so that his voice carried to everyone present, 'and the main one is, you keep your mouth shut no matter what.' There was a dangerous tone in the manner in which he said this, which was reflected in the silence and the attitude of the others present. For a moment nobody stirred. Colin thought that if this leader remained on top of that rock for much longer without drying himself he was soon going to start to feel pretty chilly.

'Well, I have heard that somebody has been speaking out of turn. It was yesterday in the grocer's shop. Somebody opened his big mouth and talked about the boat in a way which might have shown that he knew what it was used for —and that's one of our secrets and nobody else is to know, or even guess. He also, for good measure, mentioned these meetings. He said too much, and he talked like this when there were strangers in that shop, who might have been anybody for all he knew.'

There was another little struggle on the rocks to the right of Colin and Fred, and it appeared that two of the boys were holding another one between them.

'It was an accident,' called the struggling boy. 'It just slipped out.'

'Like his bottom out of his bathers last week,' said another, 'when he was in the sea when all them tourists were about.'

The chuckle which temporarily relieved the tension stopped almost as soon as it had begun, and there was silence again.

'You were showing off,' said the dark-haired boy with a tone of disgust, 'trying to make yourself look important. Trying to hint at things, even if you weren't saying outright what the things were. Just to make people curious and make yourself look big.'

'I wasn't,' denied the boy who had ceased struggling for the moment. His face was still in the light of the sunset, but it was pale. 'It was just an accident.'

'There's a punishment for talking,' declared Derek evenly and slowly, 'even "by accident". We don't allow anyone to talk like that; it might cause trouble.' There was a definitely evil sound to the sneer in his voice, as if he enjoyed threatening and punishing those smaller than himself. Colin remembered the Chinese burn which he had inflicted upon him. 'Bring him up here!'

Two boys, one on either side of the victim, began to drag him up the uneven slope of the rocks towards the pinnacle.

To say that the victim was not willing would be an under-statement.

'Simon,' called Derek softly, 'if you struggle like that you might fall off the ledge, and that would be nasty, wouldn't it?'

Simon paused momentarily and looked down at the pool beneath him, and to Colin's surprise burst into tears. He imagined that Derek had in mind the infliction of another twisting of the flesh, or maybe even bending him over the rock in full view of everyone else and whacking him with a stick or something. Simon seemed too old to cry, especially since it seemed clear that he was crying in terror. It might be embarrassing to be spanked, Chinese-burned or otherwise thumped while everyone was watching, but he couldn't see how terror came into it at all. If he had been the one being dragged up there, Colin thought grimly, he would make sure that he gave a good account of himself, whether Derek was a nasty piece of work or not.

The three boys reached the pinnacle and at once Derek stood on one side and the dark-haired boy on the other, so that Simon could not escape. The light was going fast. Colin shivered and realized that Fred was also feeling the cold and was hunching himself together. There was a large mole in the centre of Fred's back which he noticed for the first time as he bent forward. It looked black on the tanned skin. Below them, the water looked unpleasant now, and it was still not very deep.

'Now you've seen me dive in just now, haven't you?' demanded Derek.

Simon could be seen nodding fearfully.

'And I came out again safely and straight away, didn't I?' Derek seemed to be asking everyone who was present to con-firm this, and there was a nodding of heads in agreement from the others. 'So it's quite safe, isn't it?' he further demanded. 'Isn't it?' he shouted, and everyone shouted back: 'Yes!' The shout was more of a mumble, but it seemed to satisfy him.

More terror took over Simon, and he shook as he sobbed. 'No, Derek, please,' he pleaded. 'I can't.'

'You're going to,' said Derek from between teeth which seemed to be clenched together in a kind of smirk.

'No—Derek!' screeched the boy. The sound was a sudden shock in the air.

The leader and the dark-haired boy seized Simon's arms and lowered him, kicking and struggling, to the ledge beneath. Because he was still kicking they let him dangle until his feet were below the level of the ledge and were hanging in space. Then he hung still, in a panic, stretched out fully with his arms straight up into the air and his legs stiffly below him. They raised him until his feet were resting on the ledge, then when he was quite upright they let go and he was on his own.

'Now dive into the water,' ordered Derek with menace in his voice.

'I can't! I daren't!'

'Dive or be pushed,' grinned the dark-haired one, making a move towards the figure on the ledge.

Simon's eyes rolled a little, then he seemed to recover himself just a little and looked at the water below. Derek inspected the assembly, and his eyes caught sight of Colin and Fred.

'Fred Pope and Ginger, get into the water to recover *the body,*' he said.

Colin found himself in the cold water with Fred and swimming quickly towards the table rock, which they climbed upon and sat waiting. He didn't know why he should have obeyed, but perhaps it was because as a stranger he could not be held as responsible as those who lived there permanently. Anyway, surely the kid wouldn't die just by diving into the pool? Though it did seem pretty shallow still.

'Move!' shouted Derek in a rage, and Simon sniffed back a few more tears and dived in.

It was a bit too dark, that was it. It was not so bad actually in the water, but from the pinnacle it would have looked very black down there. Simon came down and Colin winced as he saw the right shoulder strike a protruding corner of the table of rock. Simon had misjudged the point of entry, or did not know where it was. When he came to the surface he was crying again—moaning softly all the time. Fred and Colin slid into the water beside him, and it was obvious that he could not move his right arm at all.

They helped him out towards this nearest edge of the rocks, but he just sat on the lowest rocks rocking backwards and forwards and moaning and holding his right elbow with his left hand. He looked misshapen across the right-hand top of his chest. Colin and Fred sat down on either side of him and tried to comfort him a little while they thought of what they ought to do.

'Seems a bit harsh, eh, Ginger?' called Derek, still on the pinnacle and seemingly unwilling to descend. 'Well, that's the sort of thing that happens to those who tell tales. And if you're thinking that it'll be safe for you to talk when you get home, let me tell you that we have friends in Birmingham as well.'

Colin was startled. Who had told Derek where he came from? And how dare he threaten him! He knew the universal code of all schoolboys: 'You shall not tell tales.' Well, there might be an exception, if someone was stealing, and that was about all.

'This is all your fault,' he stormed at the figure on the rock. 'What are you going to do about him now?'

Derek ignored him. 'Pope,' he called from the height, 'you're next on the boat trip. And no one had better talk about it.'

Then he turned and stepped off the rocks and passed from view. The rest of the boys also either climbed off the rocks and hurriedly changed into their clothes, or a few gathered round Fred, Colin and Simon.

'Well, it was your own fault, Si,' said one.

Simon nodded miserably as if he agreed.

Another turned to Colin. 'He's lucky. The last one who talked, he didn't talk again.'

'What happened?'

'Fell off the cliff.' He said it in such a matter-of-fact way.

'I don't see,' said Colin in amazement, 'how you put up with it. You're all stupid. Why do you let Derek get away with it? He must be mad.'

'You did as he told you, didn't you?' said the first pointedly.

'I didn't know what was going to happen.'

'Well, there are other reasons,' said the second vaguely, and would not explain further.

'We can't stay here all night,' said Colin. 'We'll have to get him home. And we'll have to get dry first.'

Only Fred and himself were left, for the others had slipped away to change, and then presumably go to their various homes, as if ashamed to be found there.

'Come on.'

Simon stumbled with them to where his clothes were laid, and they dried him first, gently, and dressed him as well as they could. He could not bear pressure on his shoulder or right arm, so Colin rightly surmised that the impact had broken his collar bone, especially as he could see where a lump rose under the skin. When Simon was ready and seated on a dry part of the beach, Colin and Fred attended to themselves, and then they helped the casualty up the steps and along the cliff path to the village.

Of course Fred knew where Simon lived, so they took him home and knocked on the door. A tall man, presumably Simon's father, opened it.

'I'm afraid Simon's had an accident,' said Colin cautiously.

'Oh? Come in. What happened, then?' As least he was not making a fuss.

His mother appeared and gave a little clutch to her breath as she inspected her son, and then chuntered on about how he ought not to be so foolish when it was getting dark, and went to fetch some bandages. Colin hoped that she knew what she was doing.

When they left, Simon's father was setting off to the telephone box in the village to ring for an ambulance. Colin felt a little guilty, but hoped that it did not show.

At the crossroads near the church: 'What did Derek mean, it was your turn next on the boat trip?' asked Colin bluntly.

Fred put one finger alongside his nose. 'Tomorrow night. Just a little job we do,' he said. 'Nobody is supposed to tell, but you'll know soon enough if you're picked. There's nothing to it. It's not really dangerous or anything.'

'If nobody's supposed to tell, how do *you* know?' asked Colin.

Fred looked down at his shoes. 'We all know. It's just—well—I don't want to make you too involved. I'll tell you after, if you like. I mean, we're mates, aren't we?'

And that was all that Colin could get out of him.

FOUR

THE PRETEND ARTIST

His mother was cutting sandwiches when he arrived at Aunt Daphne's for breakfast, and packing them in greaseproof paper and laying them into a small plastic box.

'The bus goes at ten,' she said, 'so you'll have to get a move on.'

'Where're we going?' he asked.

'St Ives.'

'I've decided to take your mother out for the day,' said Aunt Daphne expansively. She was not sitting in her chair this time, but on the edge of her bed with her broken leg, the white plaster concealed under a brown stocking, straight out in front of her, and putting a large black comb through her hair. In her mouth she held a couple of hair-grips, which did not seem to affect her speech in the slightest. 'And you ought to see the local sights as well, while you have the chance. It's good for your education to widen your knowledge of places by doing a little travelling.'

So saying, she popped the hair-grips into her hair, struggled to her feet and wobbled to examine her appearance in the mirror.

'Besides,' she continued when she had made a few final adjustments and seemed satisfied, 'I have an old friend in St Ives whom I haven't seen for a very long time. She'll think I'm dead, and I'm going to prove to her that I'm not. Now hurry up with the breakfast, and don't dawdle. The washing-up will be waiting for you.'

St Ives was a queer place in a pleasant kind of way. Since it was holiday time, it was full of visitors, but what struck Colin especially was the small number of cars in the town.

'It's because visitors aren't allowed to bring their cars in,' said his aunt, as the three of them passed into a narrow alley leading from one of the streets to the tiny house where his great-aunt's friend lived. 'It's residents only here, young man. Tourists have to park on the big car park right at the top of the hill, and then walk. And quite right, too. Now are you coming in, or would you rather go off by yourself? I'm going to talk, your mother's going to talk, then later, we shall have a meal and look at the shops. You might find it more interesting to go and enjoy yourself in the sun.'

Her youngest relation said he would rather look around, if nobody would mind. Aunt Daphne said that was what they had thought, and the sandwiches were for him. She and his mother would use a restaurant. Then she looked at him thoughtfully, and dived into her handbag without even swaying. She was an expert at using crutches now, he noticed. 'You'd better have some spending money,' she remarked gruffly, and handed him a pound note. 'Don't lose it or spend it stupidly. Now help me up the steps, Mary, and ring the bell. We are expected. You know what time to come back,' she called after Colin. 'Don't be late, or we'll miss the bus.'

The sea front and the harbour were the biggest attractions to Colin. He ate his sandwiches sitting on the edge of the harbour and dangling his legs over the side, while the hungry gulls screamed overhead.

It was while he was exploring the town that he came across an artist's studio which was open to the public. Nobody was trying to sell anything, so he joined the handful of people inside and looked at the paintings hanging on the wall with price labels attached. The artist himself, a curved pipe in his mouth, was working at an easel in one corner, surrounded by trestle tables on which paints were spread out in some confusion. By the time he reached the easel the artist had gone, so he inspected the picture on which he had been working.

It was a dark landscape, with storm clouds over a cottage on moorland and two trees near the cottage, and a striking bright light appearing in the clouds and stretching down over one side of the cottage walls. Very effective, he thought, but not the sort of thing he would like to buy—even if he could have afforded it. The paint, which had been applied with a pallet knife, not a brush, was not yet dry.

He turned his attention to other pictures round the studio. He was not impressed by any of them, he had to confess to himself—only the almost-finished one on the easel. When he turned back again, in the doorway of an inner room he saw the outline of the man who had lost his gold ring on the beach, talking to the artist. They were shaking hands as if they had come to some agreement, then the door opened wider and both walked out of the studio carrying rectangular objects of varying sizes covered with brown paper and string, and laid them on the floor of a plain green van parked out-tide. Between them they must have taken about eight of them to the van.

Then the two men returned to the studio, and stood by the easel, and while Colin could not catch what was said, standing as he was on the other side of the room, his friend of the gold ring pointed at the unfinished picture. The artist had a doubtful expression and removing his pipe chewed his lip a little, but finally nodded his head very slowly once, removed the picture from its stand and took it inside the other room with him, the second man following. In a few moments they both emerged, the one whom Colin had met before carrying two pictures, one wrapped in paper and the other the one he had just seen on the easel, which was too wet to be wrapped up.

What occurred next was even more surprising, for a traffic warden was standing by the van and was taking out his pad and pencil. The man from the beach strolled round to the

44

warden, extracted a small leather wallet from his rear pocket of his jeans and held it close to the warden's face. Colin nipped out of the studio to watch. The warden inspected the card carefully, stepped back a pace, nodded and wandered off, replacing his pad as he went. The van had been parked on double yellow lines which ran the whole length of the road. Perhaps the man with the small bald patch was a resident of St Ives, concluded Colin—but somehow that did not fit with what the man had told him previously. It was still odd.

It was growing late enough for him to make his way back to the house where his great-aunt's friend lived, but on the way he paused at the lifeboat station to have a look at the boat. When he had climbed down the steps from the visitors' catwalk and emerged into the street again, he saw by the harbour, talking to a boatman, Mr Trewan, just a few yards away. He had the impression that he, too, was coming to an arrangement of some kind. He waved his hand cheerfully at Mr Trewan, to show that he had seen him, but Mr Trewan looked through him, then studiously turned the other way. He must have noticed, Colin concluded, because he had turned in the direction of the waving arm, but very likely he had not recognized him. He scurried on to the house in the narrow alley, wondering how when people moved house they managed to get the furniture in or out in those narrow places.

They got Aunt Daphne home safely, grumbling that her crutches were a plain nuisance and that she was going to use a thick walking-stick instead at the earliest opportunity. The reason was probably that the bus had been delayed while she climbed out of it and she didn't relish being addressed as an 'old girl', in no matter how friendly a fashion, by the driver who had come round to assist her. His mother had been out shopping during the course of the day but had bought only a tea towel decorated with a map of Cornwall, and one with next year's calendar printed on it. She gave the calendar tea towel to Aunt Daphne, who was clearly pleased with the gift but pretended that she thought her niece had wasted her money.

After tea, Colin discovered Fred at the village crossroads, and asked if he would be going down to the cove.

'You'd better not come with me,' said Fred seriously. 'Remember?'

Colin remembered. 'Be seeing you, then,' he said, and while Fred set off towards Geraint's Cove leaned like a local boy against the signpost. Then after a few moments a thought struck him and he walked briskly down the hill in the same direction as Fred had taken. When he reached the turn where the cliff path led off from the road, he continued towards the harbour instead, for he had in his mind an idea of what he might find happening there.

The public house on the edge of the harbour was doing a good trade. *The Six Lobsters* it was called. Through the open windows he could hear the noise of music mingled with laughter and a great deal of conversation, for the public rooms were full. In the harbour boats bobbed at their moorings. The tide did not recede far enough at any time, it seemed, to leave the harbour so empty of water that boats were left high and dry, and the larger boat which took trippers on excursions was still there.

On board, however, there was some activity. It had taken him about ten minutes or so to reach the harbour, Colin estimated, and Fred had left the village perhaps five minutes prior to that. So Fred would easily be down at the cove by now. He took a walk to the very end of the harbour, where a path led to some rocks, and there he sat and waited for what he guessed was likely to take place. From here, he could not see the cove, because it was well out of sight somewhere over to his right about half a mile or maybe a little farther, so he would not be able to observe anything taking place there. What happened in the cove, however, was not what he intended to watch to see if his theory was the right one.

Then he heard a boat engine start up, and sauntered to the harbour, leaned over the wall and watched. As he had expected, the trippers' boat was casting off its moorings, and there were two men on board. He did not recognize either of them. As the boat drew away, he walked briskly round so that he could keep her in sight for as long as possible. When she passed out of sight, he ran to the *Six Lobsters* and climbed the hill which rose just behind it. From the top he could watch the boat, and in a matter of minutes he caught sight of a smaller craft, perhaps a rowing dinghy, heading towards it.

It was not light enough to be certain of what was happening then, but he could still catch the sound of the boat's engine over the water, and the note of this dropped quite clearly, then after what seemed a few minutes more it picked up again and he heard it draw away towards the open sea.

Then he had been right! Fred had been picked up by the boat and no doubt by now the rowing dinghy was being towed astern, just like on the previous occasion. Thoughtfully, he descended the little hill.

Before he set off home for his supper, he took a walk along the beach, because there was the curious sight of a man who seemel to be cleaning the little beach with a vacuum cleaner. However, it was not a vacuum cleaner but a round metal disc on the end of a pole, and the man was sweeping the disc backwards and forwards in front of him as he walked slowly forward. A rapid ticking sound came from a box at his waist, and as this happened the man switched off the machine, picked up a spade and a sieve, and dug at the spot vigorously, throwing the sand into the sieve. When the sieve was half-full, he picked it up and shook it. It was the man who had lost his gold ring. He looked up to see Colin watching him.

'Hello,' he said. 'Wondering what I'm doing?'

Colin nodded.

'I'm finding buried treasure.'

47

'Dropped your ring again?' Colin wanted to know.

The man laughed. 'No, but you're not far out.' He straightened up and held out his hand. 'See that.' In his palm rested a fifty pence piece. 'People drop this sort of thing on the beach when they're on holiday.'

'But it's not yours,' said Colin.

'True, but it's not anyone else's, either. You think, some tourists come here, and they lose some money in the sand—like I lost my ring. So they sift the sand for it, and can't find it. What do they do, report the loss to the police? No, because it's not worth it, and in any case who's going to search the beach just for an odd coin? So they decide it's just hard luck and when they go away the money stays where they dropped it. Mind you, fifty pence is good going. I usually find only coppers.'

Colin considered carefully. A metal detector cost a lot of money. How could the man make it pay?

The man laughed again. 'You'd be surprised,' he said. 'On a good night I can find a pound or two which people have left behind. It makes me about five or six pounds a week, if I'm lucky, even on a beach this size.'

Colin still could not see how anyone could make a living out of it. The stranger explained that actually he was an artist, and that money-detecting was merely a side-line. 'Come on up to the pub,' he urged, 'and I'll buy you a coke out of tonight's profits. It's one pound seventy-two pence I've found this evening.'

He noticed as they sat outside the public house on a bench underneath one of the windows that the conversation consisted largely of questions about himself, and that of the stranger he was learning very little. He did discover that the man was not from Geraint's Cove, but that he was born a Cornishman, but in return the man found out that Colin's mother was a widow, what friends he had made since he had arrived, how often he visited the cove and what he did there (Colin was cagey about that, but the man did not appear to

48

notice), and then he asked why Colin had gone down to the harbour that evening.

'To try and hitch a lift on that boat which went out, I suppose,' the man suggested.

'No—no,' said Colin. 'I just came for a look round.'

'That boat goes out in the evenings every now and then, quite empty apart from a couple of men who drive it.'

'Perhaps they go fishing,' said Colin.

'Oh no. I think they just go out for the ride,' said the other.

They had finished their drinks, and Colin was asked to keep an eye on the equipment while the man returned the glasses to the bar. When he came out again, they walked up the road a little way. At the door of what looked like a disused barn but which of course could not have been that, the man stopped.

'I stay here,' he announced, unlocked the door with a yale key and switched on the light.

Here was another time to be cautious, just in case entering this building was something similar to accepting a lift in a car from a strange man, but nevertheless Colin entered. Inside, it appeared to be very much the same as the studio in St Ives, except that the pictures were leaning against the walls from the top of trestle tables, not hanging up. There were not as many as in the other studio, and the artist saw him glancing round.

'Not been here long,' he explained, 'so I've not done many yet.' He threw the cover off a picture which stood on an easel. 'This is the one I'm doing now,' he added. 'There's just the finishing touch or two to add.'

It was a scene of a cottage on a moorland, with storm clouds overhead, and Colin recognized it instantly as the one which had been on an easel in St Ives that same afternoon. The difference was, it had been quite another artist who had been painting it then. This man was either a liar or a fake, he was not sure which.

'It's simple, you see,' the man was going on. 'If I paint pictures here, people can come in and see me at work, and perhaps buy one of them, but if I painted out of sight, so to speak, I'd have the bother of sending them off to art galleries and have to wait a long time for my money.'

Colin chose not to reveal what he knew, but an interesting question was forming itself in his mind and for the moment there was no way in which to find the answer. The man could not be making a living out of metal-detecting, nor by selling a few pictures which were not his. He would receive more from Social Security, or unemployment pay, or something.

'Where do you sleep?' asked Colin, looking around. He had expected to find a bed behind a curtain at least, such as Aunt Daphne had.

'Upstairs of course. Bed-sitter upstairs, work room downstairs.'

That seemed reasonable, now that he could see a small door at the end of the bare studio. Colin knew about bed-sitters.

'Anyway, I think it's time you went home,' said the artist, 'or your people will be wondering where you are—your mother or your great-aunt, I mean. But do call again and see me. I'm nearly always around the district somewhere, doing something or other. Just you, mind, not half the village. Oh, and I say,' he added as Colin was preparing to leave, 'I think it might be an idea if you didn't tell any of your friends in the village about our little chat. Don't want them all round, you know, putting me off my work.'

It was not only the dark which made the whole area seem mysterious as Colin wended his way slowly back to the village, but it was almost as if he was encountering something quite beyond his understanding. It was disturbing. There was the unusual secret rite of the village boys, who dived into that overgrown puddle of sea water and broke each others' limbs if anyone gave away their secrets. There was the boat, which seemed to be something to be kept hidden from the eyes of outsiders, almost as if it were a religious symbol. Even the few adults whom he had met had their secrets and deceptions, like Derek's father, who had denied that the boat belonged to him, and who later on must have seen him but had pretended that he had not, and like this so-called artist, who was not an artist at all. And even his great-aunt had asked sharply with which boy he had become friendly, as if there were some boys with whom it would have been undesirable to have too much contact.

It was as if Colin had found himself in the middle of a sequence of dark events which were quite at variance with the delights of the beautiful area of the country in daylight. He even jumped as a bat flew just over his head and squeaked its way across the fields on its search for food.

FIVE

STOWAWAY

'Now I know what you did,' said Colin.

'When?'

'Last night. You took the boat out of the cove, rowed it out to sea, met that boat from the harbour which is used for giving people trips along the coast, got on board, and the boat was towed behind. Then you came back.'

'You were watching,' accused Fred. 'I told you you mustn't.'

They were sitting on the church wall.

'I wasn't. I saw Derek go out in it a day or two ago, and saw what happened then. So last night I watched the other boat leave the harbour and the rowing boat met it. You were the one in the rowing boat.'

Fred supposed that he was.

'But what do you do? I mean, you row out, you meet this boat, you go out to sea. Then what do you do?'

Fred looked embarrassed, and said that they did nothing. That was it, he had rowed out, got on board the other boat, they had tied the rowing boat to the stern, gone out to sea, and then returned. Colin did not believe him.

'Well, that's it,' flared Fred. 'We didn't do anything else.'

Colin was incredulous, because it didn't make sense and he couldn't see the point of it. 'If they wanted to give you a ride in a boat, why couldn't you go down to the harbour and get on board there?' he demanded.

Fred shook his head and said that Colin didn't understand.

There were reasons, he added darkly, why it had to be done as it was, and it might be that Colin would find out soon enough—or he might not. Really it might be better if he did not, he implied.

'But what's the point of it all?' asked Colin. 'Do you really know, yourself?'

'Oh, I know all right,' said Fred, but would not be drawn further. It was almost as if he were trying to protect Colin from something, but whatever it was, Fred himself did not seem to be any the worse for it. Then a number of other boys turned up and a game of cricket was improvised in the field behind the church for the rest of the morning, and in the afternoon about half of that number went down to the beach to play. In the strong, clear sunlight it was a most enjoyable day, and Colin pitied the visitors with such a short time to appreciate it before they had to return to their factories and offices and land-locked streets. Out here, even work or attending school would seem like a permanent holiday, if he lived there all the time.

Fred went off to see to the cows about four o'clock, and a number of other boys seemed to have similar tasks, for they left until finally there was only the dark-haired boy, Colin and perhaps three others among the holidaymakers on the beach, and then they decided it was time to go as well. As they passed the café, Derek appeared at the top of the rough steps which led up to it, and called.

'Hey, Mark.'

The dark-haired boy turned. So at last Colin knew his name.

'What?'

'Your turn.'

'Okay.'

'Your turn to do what?' enquired Colin. 'The usual?' He added somewhat maliciously.

Although Mark, at the meeting by the pool, seemed to be a sinister second-in-command, in daylight he was quite different; a bit moody, perhaps, and with strangers rarely to smile, but Colin had noticed that during the afternoon he had a considerable sense of fun. When he smiled he looked a totally different character. This time, he did smile. 'You know too much,' he said, 'but as long as you keep it to yourself, you'll do all right. It just means I'm taking the boat out tonight. Derek works out a sort of list of those who are suitable, and when you're told, you go.'

'How does he decide who's suitable, then?'

Mark looked him over. 'You've got to be old enough,' he said, 'and strong enough to row. You have to be old enough so's you don't panic.'

'What do they do to you?'

Mark looked at him queerly. 'They don't do anything to you. What do you think they are? All you have to do is what you're told, and that's all there is to it. Most of the time you just sit there.'

'But where does the boat go?'

'Just out to sea and back. Doesn't take long.'

It was while he was performing his duty of washing-up after tea that Colin thought of something which might be useful, if he were to find some sort of solution to the mystery. He asked his great-aunt if she possessed such a thing as a pair of binoculars. She looked at him quizzically, as if weighing up whether he were trustworthy enough, before answering.

'If you go upstairs and look behind my dressing-table, you might find a pair in a brown leather case,' she said at length. 'Don't break them.'

When he found them, where she had said on the floor in a corner of the room, he saw the letters *W. Johnson* tooled on to the case in gold. Presumably they had once belonged to his great-uncle, which was why she was being so cautious. He took them out of the case and examined them. They were large field-glasses, with an arrow and the date—1934— stamped on them, so either his great-uncle had bought them second-hand or he had been in one of the Forces, possibly as a regular officer, in that year. He would have to ask his mother sometimes what his great-uncle had done for a living. They looked like Naval glasses, so Aunt Daphne's husband might have been in the Royal Navy, because they were so large.

'I believe they are really night-glasses,' Aunt Daphne told him when he took them carefully downstairs. 'That is, they don't work in the dark, of course, but the lenses are so big so that they can catch as much of the light as possible. That's so you can use them when it isn't full daylight, and still see.'

He borrowed them for the evening. He said he wanted to see if he could follow a bat with them. His great-aunt laughed and said that he could try, but bats moved too quickly, and also they darted about. 'You know—missing the pure loop', as D. H. Lawrence said in his poem about bats.' Colin did not know, but that mattered not at all. It was not bats he was after anyway.

Walking briskly down to the harbour, he climbed the hill behind the *Six Lobsters* and waited. Down at the sandy fringe of the water, he could see the artist out with his metal detector, but he did not see Colin. Then he heard the boat's engine start up, run for a sufficiently long time to warm up, and saw the boat leave the harbour with its usual complement of two on board. When this happened, he focused the glasses and peered out to sea through them, sweeping as near to the coast as he was able until he caught sight of the rowing boat.

The glasses were magnificent. Although it was growing dusk, the magnification revealed clearly the boat and a figure in it, who appeared to be Mark, rowing steadily seawards. Slowly, it seemed, the two craft headed towards each other until at a point which might have been half a mile off the coast—Colin ought to have been able to have calculated fairly accurately, because one lens of the glasses had markings on it which indicated distance somehow, but he had no idea of how to use these markings—the launch cut its engine and drifted for a minute or two while the rowing boat came alongside. He saw Mark stand up in the rowing boat and one of those on the bigger boat reach out a hand to help him up.

Then Mark disappeared, and there was just the rowing boat, drifting a few feet away, and the man with his head over the side of the larger boat looking for him. The second man joined him. Mark came into view at once, or at least his head did, for he must have missed his footing and slipped into the water. It looked as if he was trying to get on board, but without being able to hear anything at all of the little drama Colin could make out from the gestures, which looked a little angry rather than worried, that the boy was to rescue the rowing dinghy first.

This Mark did, was helped on board properly this time, and the dinghy was pulled round to the stern by one of the two men. It seemed then, although it was now too dark and too far for Colin to be absolutely sure, that Mark went below into a cabin or something, no doubt to dry off. And then it was too dark to see anything more at all, and Colin came down the hill just in time to encounter the artist who with detector, spade and sieve was passing the public house.

'Hello there,' said the artist cheerily. 'Been watching the gulls?'

Colin fiddled with the fastening on the leather case. 'Just looking around,' he said.

'They looked a good pair, judging from the quality of the case,' declared the artist. 'May I have a look through them?'

There was no point in refusing, and the man extracted the glasses, put them to his eyes, focused them and peered out to sea, then along the top of the cliffs. Finally he nodded and examined the glasses all over before handing them back.

'A very good pair,' he announced, 'your great-aunt's, I suppose.'

56

It was not a question at all, but a simple statement which told Colin that this man remembered a great deal which other people might not have remembered. 'Anything interesting happening out at sea?' he asked suddenly.

'I just happened to catch sight of the boat which left the harbour some time back,' said Colin carelessly, 'but of course it was too dark to see much. I think I came out at the wrong time of day to use field glasses.'

'You should have seen more than that,' said the man quietly, 'because these are night glasses, designed for use when it's getting dark. Were you looking for anything in particular?' he pressed.

Hurriedly, Colin shook his head. 'Find much this evening?' he asked to change the subject from dangerous ground. The artist said he had not and he would have to leave Colin at that point and add a few touches to his latest masterpiece.

The man then wandered off towards his studio, leaving Colin at the side of the harbour, as if he had no more interest in him. Colin had expected another coke at least, but perhaps it was because the night's takings on the beach had been so small. On the other hand, perhaps it was not that at all, for as he set off towards the village he saw the artist's green van suddenly draw away from the harbour, and its tail lights disappeared in what seemed a matter of seconds round the first bend in the road, and when he passed the studio it was in total darkness.

The next morning Mark was not helpful at all, when Colin came across him coming out of one of the village shops.

'I hear you got wet last night,' remarked Colin.

'How did you hear that?' asked Mark sharply.

'Oh—I just heard.'

There was a pause. 'You'd better be careful what you hear,' said Mark with almost as much menace in his voice as if it had been Derek speaking, or as if Mark had reverted to his official capacity at one of the meetings.

57

Colin had not seen Fred that morning, so he might have been helping at the farm, and instead he asked Mark if there was to be a meeting at the cove.

'Not tonight,' said Mark. 'Nobody will go there tonight.'

'But it's Saturday,' said Colin. 'Tourists will have gone home, and the new ones won't have found the cove yet. I'd have thought it the ideal time, with nobody likely to be around apart from us.'

'Er—no.' Mark had recovered his good humour at once. 'That's it, of course. It's Saturday, so a lot leave the village for Penzance and there's no point in a meeting when there would be—er—not many of us. So nobody goes to the cove tonight,' he emphasized, almost as if telling him not to, 'not once it begins to get dark, anyway.'

And that was all Colin could get out of him, but he could sense that there was more to what Mark was telling him than met the eye. It was like weighing up a new teacher. There is a kind of instinct about it which adults tend to lose.

The next thing was that his great-aunt's toes began to turn blue, where they protruded from the lower end of the plaster of Paris which encased her broken leg. By midday, when Colin had returned to the house, he found his mother and Aunt Daphne in earnest consultation. Aunt Daphne was seated in the big chair peering at her outstretched leg where her toes were visible.

'What colour do you call my toes?' his great-aunt asked without preamble. 'Stand out of the light, Mary, and let the boy see.'

Colin obediently bent down to look. The old woman's toes were a little dirty, but that was to be expected, because if she had washed them very carefully the water would have softened the plaster, and that would have been no good at all. He looked up and stated that in his opinion they were a little bit bruised.

Aunt Daphne grunted as if that was the sort of thing she had expected to happen all along. 'No peace for the wicked,' she said, 'but I'm not going without my dinner, blue toes or no blue toes.'

'What do bruised-looking toes mean?' asked Colin.

'It means,' said his aunt ponderously, 'that some fool at the hospital has put this plaster on my leg too tightly, and now I shall have to go there yet again while they take it off and replace it.'

'You mean, with a wooden leg?' asked Colin, looking the picture of innocence but spoiling the effect by smiling too much. 'Perhaps they'll let you keep the old one to put on the mantelpiece as a souvenir.'

His great-aunt ceased to be ponderous at once. 'I'll tell them that's what I want,' she said, and there was no doubt that she didn't mean a word of it. 'I think your mother ought to be the one to go and telephone that ridiculous hospital, and they'll have to come and fetch me. What a waste of public money, having to send an ambulance all this way for such a little thing!'

His mother remonstrated that this could have happened to anybody, and it was hardly the fault of the hospital if the hot weather had caused Aunt Daphne's legs to swell. When she returned from the village telephone kiosk she said that the ambulance would be arriving at about four o'clock, and then they would have to wait in Penzance until one could be made available to take Aunt Daphne home again.

'Then that's it,' snorted the great-aunt. 'I'll go by myself. There's no need for you to waste an afternoon and most of the evening as well. You know how long you have to wait in these places, what with one thing and another.'

It was now Colin's mother's turn to be adamant and insist that she should accompany her. 'The only thing, Colin,' she warned, 'is that we might be away for a long time. So I think that what I'll do is stay with Aunt Daphne overnight. That means you'll be in the cottage by yourself, but that shouldn't bother you. There's the television, so you'll have something to do. So I'll leave you enough for your tea, and

59

something for your supper, and you must go to bed at a reasonable time.'

When Colin's mother had made up her mind, that was the end of the matter as far as Colin was concerned, and it was pointless to argue, as he knew from long experience. Thus when the ambulance arrived, half an hour later than expected, to take a grumbling patient and her niece away, he knew that he was now on his own for the rest of the night and that he might as well make the best of it. Now the opportunity had arisen, he knew what he intended to do.

It was almost dark when he hurried out of the cottage and found the cliff path. He ran down to the cove, but exercised caution as he passed under the rock platform upon which stood the café. He had thought of taking the way right through the village and then the road which led directly to the cove, but he realized that to do that would mean eventually finding himself not far from the rear of the café, and he did not want to encounter Derek, or his father.

There was nobody about anywhere on the beach as far as he could see when he turned into the first cave, then the dark passage, and then peered extremely carefully round the end of the passage into the boat cave. He tiptoed over to the boat and stood irresolute. Like the plans of most boys, his had been fine as far as they went, but he had not foreseen far enough ahead and taken care of the details. He stepped back towards the passage, and as he retreated carefully scrabbled out his footprints with his hand, then retreated right out of the cave until he was standing at the far side of its entrance. Then he crouched down on the sand and waited. That was not very clever, he thought as he sat on his haunches there, because if anyone came out of the cave he would be seen, but he could always scramble among the rocks if he heard anyone, and he was wearing his plimsolls so his feet would make no sound.

Nearly ten minutes later he caught the sound of voices, which he recognized at once as belonging to Mark and Derek.

They were coming down the passage. He stood up and flattened himself against the rock wall, then he heard Mark ask if the tarpaulin was to be left in the cave.

'Not likely,' he heard Derek reply. 'That goes in the boat, as usual. Oh, look at that. Some kids have put some rocks right across the edge of the sea. Dump the cover in the boat, then we'll go and shift them first.'

From where he stood, Colin saw the rocks to which the other had referred, a row of black stones standing at the water's edge which would have prevented the boat from being dragged smoothly into the water. He withdrew further away, then as Derek and Mark both emerged and strode purposefully to move the offending rocks, he darted back into the cave without their seeing him. The tarpaulin cover was pushed half-under the lip which ran across the bows of the rowing dinghy, and it was so dark at the back of the cave that he could not possibly be seen. He stepped inside the boat, pulled out a corner of the tarpaulin, and laid himself down underneath it, completely hidden from sight.

Derek and Mark returned and at once dragged the boat until he heard water lapping gently just by his head. Then the dragging stopped, and the next sound was a bumping at the other end of the dinghy, as if a heavy object were hitting it.

'Now you're sure you know how to operate this?' he heard Derek ask. There must have been some kind of sign in response, perhaps a nod of the head, because he continued : 'The important thing is you must lift it up as you come ashore, or the propeller could be damaged. You press the handle right down.'

'I know,' said Mark, somewhat irritably, and the boat rocked slightly as he stepped on board, and they were fully afloat.

Then an outboard motor roared, coughed and stopped again. From underneath the canvas the words came not very distinctly, but Colin caught the advice that Mark should have pulled the choke out. This time the engine started, and continued to run, the note of the engine dropped a few tones, and they were off. This was faster travel than rowing could have achieved. The question still uppermost in Colin's mind was why the journey was being made at all, and that was what he was there to find out. He hoped that no part of his body was showing, especially his feet, and in the darkness took the liberty of huddling himself into a smaller space, expecting that Mark would be too busy operating the engine to notice.

He heard nothing of the sound of another boat's engine, but he knew when the dinghy slowed down that they had reached the first objective. There was a heavy rocking motion as somebody either climbed into the dinghy or climbed out.

'Where's Derek, then?' he heard a man's voice say quite loudly.

'Caught some fingers in the counter shelf,' Mark replied, 'so didn't like to risk it.'

'Clumsy oaf.'

Then there was a moment's stillness, and afterwards the dinghy moved a little, stopped, then set off again at a rather faster speed, heading heaven knew where. Colin decided that this was the point at which the dinghy was being towed by the larger craft.

They travelled for some considerable time, and while he did not possess a watch he judged it must have been nearly another half hour before the speed reduced and then the forward motion ceased altogether, leaving the dingy rolling in the sea. There was a thump which reverberated through the woodwork as someone heavy came into the boat. It was certainly not Mark. He felt a movement under his left foot, and very slowly raised it. His foot had been resting on the blade of one of the oars, which this other person was now removing. Creaking rowlocks indicated that the dinghy was now being rowed, but it was for a very short distance, then whoever it had been climbed out, and there was silence as far as the boy could tell.

He risked drawing back the canvas a little, but could see and hear nothing. It was certain that he was alone in the boat, so he risked further pulling back the tarapulin and raising his head, with difficulty, to peer over the side so that just his eyes were above the level of the gunwale.

He was alongside a completely different boat now, with a little step-ladder hanging over the side. It was a much larger boat, too. Looking across the water, he could just make out the dim outline of the tripper's launch, and there was not a light to be seen in any direction. Then there were footsteps on the boat's decking just above his head, and he caught the words: *'Eh bien, monsieur.'* At that point he ducked down into hiding once more, as the heavy man stepped down, and for the next minute or two the boat rocked considerably as he felt objects of some sort being carried into the dinghy.

'Assez,' he heard vaguely, and knew enough French from what he had learned at school to know that a Frenchman was saying: 'Enough.'

The dinghy was rowed a short distance, there was a bump as it touched, then whatever had been loaded into the dinghy was unloaded. Whatever they were, they were heavy, he was sure of that, for he could feel the dinghy rise a little out of the water as they were taken off.

Three times the process was repeated, then there was a pause, the dinghy seemed to be hitched to the English boat once more, and he could feel himself turning round in a wide circle. Half an hour later two people climbed into the dinghy and loaded it, the outboard motor started, and after a short time the nose of the dinghy grounded on sand. He heard the outboard whine a little, presumably as Mark had raised it from the water during the last few yards. Then the boat emptied—he assumed—and temporarily there was silence.

He lifted his head and could see no one, but he sensed movement in the cave where the boat was normally kept. Slipping out over the side and keeping to one side of the dinghy he found his feet in water. The dinghy was almost broadside to the cave, which was perhaps, Colin decided, a good thing if he was not to be seen. Now to make some kind of getaway without being spotted, for he now had a pretty good idea of just what was going on and considered that it might be very dangerous to be discovered. If boys' arms and legs were broken just for speaking accidentally out of turn, the punishment for being found in the wrong place would be, he judged, possibly something more permanent than that, and he had not any intention at all of being caught in such a compromising situation.

A panic which made his heart thump wildly took over him as he ran, crouching low so as not to be seen even in that darkness, not in the direction of the pool, where he could hear water splashing since the tide was almost full, but in the opposite direction and nearer to the first of the two joined caves.

He ran silently and swiftly, doubled up as he was, to the nearest rock pile, and there he subsided quickly, trying to prevent his gasps for breath from becoming audible, hidden between two rocks. He determined to wait there for a while. He ought to be safe, for there was far more on the larger boat than had been brought ashore on this trip. It would take a minimum of two more trips to unload, and when the dinghy set off again would be the time to hurry off the beach and get back to the cottage.

It was then that he caught sight of something blacker than the dark rocks surrounding him, and it was lying just next to him. As he rose to his feet to run, a hand from this dark shape clamped over his mouth and he was held firmly on the ground so that he could not move.

It was the artist.

SIX

IN THE STUDIO

For how long he was held he did not know. Certainly it was
long enough for the dinghy to set off from the shore again
until he and the man appeared to be the only humans left
on the beach. Still nothing happened to him, but Colin lay
still, petrified. Then the man leaned towards him, still with
his hand over the boy's mouth, to say quietly in his ear:

'Good evening. And what have you been up to, eh?'

It was not a voice with a sinister tone at all, which was
surprising. Perhaps the worst was yet to come.

'Now I'm going to take my hand from your mouth. Whatever you do, don't make any noise. Talk very quietly. Nod
your head if you agree.'

Colin was too frightened to do anything other, and his
face was released at once. He could still feel the pressure of
the fingers on his cheeks.

'So tell me what you are doing here, and be quick.'

'I just stowed away on the boat, to see where it went.'

'That was stupid. But you can't stay here. Anyone at
home?'

Colin shook his head, fearfully wondering why the man
had asked the question. If there was nobody at home, then
nobody else would know where he was.

'Then get off the beach—quick. But go very quietly, and if
you see anyone at all, hide straight away. No heroics, see?
Don't go home, but once you reach the road run down to my
studio, and once you're inside, lock the door, go upstairs and

make yourself comfortable. But don't switch on any lights. Here's the key.'

A yale key was pressed into his hand.

'You'll know it's me when I arrive, because I shall knock three times on the door, then I shall use my spare key. Got all that?'

'Yes,' whispered Colin, now very subdued.

'Then do exactly as I've told you. Get going, before they return. And don't fall over the cliff on your way.'

Colin needed no further urging, but rose to his feet and ran and scrambled as fast as he was able, and once he had attained the road, without incident he was glad to discover, he pelted down it regardless of the slapping noise his rubber soles were making, until he reached the first house near the harbour. Then he stopped.

There was not a soul about. Upstairs in one house he saw the curtains glowing orange from the electric light burning in a bedroom, and in two of the houses there was a downstairs light switched on. It must have been later than he had thought. He wondered if he would not be far better off going home and bolting the cottage door behind him, but to do that meant returning up the hill, and he might meet someone who would want to know why he was out and about so late. He might even come across Derek, or Mark, or even one of the men from the boat, and they could perhaps be very suspicious and possibly extremely unpleasant.

The only choice seemed to be to follow the instructions he had been given, yet if he did it was likely that the supposed artist would be the only person in the world who would have any knowledge of where he was. For all he knew, the artist was merely trapping him so that he could dispose of him later. Now that did not seem likely, because from the position of the artist as he had hid on the beach he had no connection with the others, who were almost certainly smuggling something ashore which they didn't want anyone else to know about. The artist, that is, was probably spying on them, and was most likely just as surprised as he had been when they had come across each other between the rocks.

So having no real choice at all, he padded off to the door of the studio, unlocked it, slipped within like a shadow and as he closed the door behind him as gently as he could heard the lock click as it slid back into place.

It was very dark indeed inside, and he had to remember in time that the artist had warned him not to switch on any lights, so he felt his way along until he arrived at the door at the end of the large downstairs room and found wooden stairs leading upwards. He climbed cautiously until he saw just above him a red glow. There was a second door part-open at the head of the stairs, and the glow was from an electric fire inside a small room.

After the darkness his eyes had grown used to the dark and by the dim light of the fire he could see that he was in a kind of untidy bedroom, with a camp bed alongside one wall, a plain wooden table underneath the window across which a brown curtain was now drawn, an armchair in the far corner nearest to the electric fire, and in a corner of the room next to the armchair a wash-basin with soap and towel, and on it a glass containing a toothbrush and a part-used tube of toothpaste. On the table were a few odd items such as a hair brush, some writing paper and a ballpoint pen. There was an old carpet on the floor, with what looked like a new rug lying nearest to the camp bed because it had a much cleaner appearance. On the floor against one of the walls stood an electric kettle, a tiny electric cooker, and some cups, saucers and plates in plain white. Presumably the cutlery was in a drawer in the table, but he did not look to see.

He sank into the armchair wearily and kept his face to-wards the door in apprehension. He was surprised how tired he felt, and how cold he had become, and was grateful for the fire. He reached over and switched on an extra bar to provide more warmth. He had to keep awake, for he had no means at all of knowing what was going to happen next. He had to listen for three knocks on the door, so he could be sure it was the artist who was coming in and not somebody else. He had also to be awake just in case the artist was not on his side at all, even if he was actually going to be the next to come in through that door. After all, there must be some reason why he had been told that he must not switch on any lights. He thought that in the distance he heard a bang, like someone slamming a door, or a car back-firing.

When he awoke, he was in bed. But it was the wrong bed. It was too narrow, and instead of being in his pyjamas he was in his underpants. He looked around him. There was daylight in the room, but it seemed a cold kind of light, and at the washbasin he could see the artist, with his shirt off, who seemed to be pressing the fleshy part of his left upper arm with a wad of white lint.

'What—' he began.

The artist turned at once. 'Hello, kid. Had a good sleep?' Then he continued to press on his arm.

'What time is it?'

The artist glanced at a watch which lay on the table.

'About a quarter to six.'

'What are you doing?'

'Got a little scratch which started to bleed again, but I think it's stopped now.' He twisted his arm round carefully and examined it. 'Yes, it's stopped. Any good at applying a bandage?'

Colin noticed that on the floor lay a shirt with a patch of blood on it which was drying brown. He climbed out of the bed.

'I want it round here, not too tightly, but tight enough to keep a little pressure on the cut.'

The boy observed that it was a funny sort of cut. It was far too deep to be an ordinary scratch, and it ran for perhaps two inches across the arm, like an inverted red weal. He enquired how the man had managed to cut himself like that, but the artist gave him a sideways look and said that it didn't

68

matter how, as long as it didn't start to bleed again.

'Not too much thickness of bandage, now,' he ordered. 'I don't want any sign of an injury when I put a shirt on again.'

'Why not?'

'Bad for business. I don't want everybody to know. In fact, I'd go so far as to say that I don't want *anybody* to know, so keep your mouth firmly shut if anyone should happen to ask questions. Anyone at all—see?'

Colin nodded and completed the bandaging over a clean piece of lint, tying the end round the man's arm.

'Now tell me what you did last night,' resumed the artist when the operation was completed. 'When I came back, you were dog-tired and asleep in the chair, so I undressed you and tucked you into the bed. You never even stirred.'

'Where did you sleep?'

'In the chair, of course. Now tell me all about last night.'

Colin said that he couldn't. Since he was up and fully awake now, he began to put on his clothes. He said he'd got to get home. The man said that he could not just climb out of a boat in which he had obviously been hiding, run behind some rocks and hide a second time, without having taken part in some interesting experience. 'You were hiding in the boat, of course, weren't you? A very dangerous thing for you to have done.'

Colin said that he could not tell him anything, and then remained silent as he bent down to tie his laces, keeping his face averted. The man stood looking down at the crouching figure, and there might have been an expression of calculation on his face, but Colin could not see this.

'All right,' the man said at length. 'It's light, but we'll have to risk that; there won't be many people about at this time of the morning to see you. I want you to run home as fast as you can, and then go to bed to get some proper rest. I also want you to keep everything that happened last night exclusively to yourself. You must tell nobody at all, not your mother, nor your great-aunt, nor any friends—nobody. It must remain a complete secret. You never saw me, you never came here, I never saw you. Got it?'

'What are you afraid of?' asked Colin somewhat insolently now that he had recovered some of his courage.

'I'm not—it's not for me that I might be afraid,' answered the man sternly. 'But now you've got yourself into this, I'm going to let you keep the key to the studio. If you find yourself in a real emergency, then you can use it and come up here. This upstairs door has got a strong bolt on it, too. But if you don't find yourself in an emergency, then for heaven's sake don't use it. And don't let anyone else discover that you've got that key. Now you'd better go, before it's too late.'

Colin required no urging, but without a word padded down the wooden stairs, through the studio, turned the knob to unlatch the big door, and pulling that outer door behind him to lock it again ran off at a steady jog-trot up the road through the cool, clear morning light. He heard nothing but seagulls, and saw nobody. He did not wake again until ten o'clock.

SEVEN

THE BARREL IN THE BARN

'Good morning, Lie-abed,' his mother greeted him cheer-fully, when he arrived in a hurry at Aunt Daphne's. 'Have you come for breakfast or lunch?'

'The sun must have been scorching your eyes out,' said his great-aunt, equally cheerfully. She had on a very white new plaster. 'Who got to bed late, then?'

Worried, Colin asked what she meant, and wondered what she knew or had guessed at, but it turned out that she was only implying that he had sat up watching the television until late.

'Do you know how the man took my old plaster off?' demanded Aunt Daphne. 'He took a circular saw to it and ran it up my leg. I thought he was going to cut my leg off with it, and he said that if I didn't keep still he would do, too.' She chuckled, and Colin smiled at the thought of any-one giving orders to his great-aunt and finding that she obeyed them. 'There's a cotton-wool padding inside, which stops the saw from doing me any damage.'

Colin wanted to know, out of idle curiosity, at what time the two women had returned to the village. They said it was late enough, and he left it at that. What he had really wanted to discover was if his mother had been to the cottage to check that he was at home, but it seemed that his adventures were safe from discovery.

'Now when you're fully recovered,' said Aunt Daphne with only the slightest trace of sarcasm after he had eaten a bowl of cornflakes ravenously, 'I want you to go to Pope's farm and get me half a hundredweight of potatoes. You know where it is—through the gate where Fred takes the cows each evening.' She reached for a purse on the dresser, handing him a five pound note and admonishing him to bring the change.

'Mrs Johnson says she would like half a hundredweight of potatoes, please,' said Colin firmly to the man whom he took to be Mr Pope. Since Fred did not live at the farm, this must be the uncle, and he was also the man who had driven him and his mother from Penzance the day they had arrived.

'Ah. If you've got your cap, then,' the farmer said slowly, 'I'll fill it.' He smiled, and Colin realized that he had made a joke at his expense, but he was not sure how to react to this country humour.

'I remember Mrs Johnson from when I was your age. A right tartar she was then. She still is. A decent old girl, but if she says something, you do it. Like I'd better get you them spuds at once, or she'll let me know about it. Got a tongue like a horse whip when she's a mind. Come on, then.'

Mr Pope ambled off towards a large shed, and Colin accompanied him.

'How come everyone's so frightened of her?' asked Colin as they came to the wooden door which the farmer unlatched and drew open.

'We're not frightened of her, it's just that she always wants a proper job doing, like she did in school, and she's been here so long she knows everybody, and everybody knows her. And she remembers. If she gets going, she starts to remind you of things you did when you were young and foolish, and she doesn't care who hears it. So to save being embarrassed, like, not wanting everyone to know, you do what she says and pretty smart about it. Cor, I remember my dad going off to that school one day, after she'd given me the stick and I'd told him it wasn't my fault. She let fly at him with her tongue and told him—and me—that she hadn't stood any nonsense with him and wasn't going to with me, either. He soon went with his tail between his legs. She'd taught him for a bit as well, you see. I didn't half get a belting when I got home. So we'd better get you what she wants, and be quick, or I'll know about it. You'll have to wait a minute, though. I've got to weigh some more out.'

So Aunt Daphne must be very old. Now how old? If Mr Pope was getting on for forty, say he'd have been about fourteen when his father had visited the school to complain. That would have been twenty-six years ago. And she had taught his father, but perhaps not for very long. Now in his father's day children would have left school at about thirteen. If she had been getting on for twenty-five and had taught Mr Pope's father for only one year, Aunt Daphne had still reminded Mr Pope's father of events a total of fifty-one years from now. Heavens, Aunt Daphne must now be getting on for ninety! She certainly could not be less than about eighty. Perhaps it was the fresh air which kept her going.

One of his teachers at school had been telling them that he had spoken to a man who had spoken to a soldier who had fought at the Battle of Waterloo, which took place in 1815. The way it had happened was that this teacher knew a man in his nineties, who when he was a very small boy had been taken to see his grandfather, who at the time had also been in his nineties. And this grandfather had been one of the Duke of Wellington's soldiers in the battle as a very young man.

Perhaps real history is closer than people usually believe. If all the members of that family were long-lived, this soldier could have spoken to his grandfather who would have died in the early part of the eighteenth century, and his grandfather would have been alive in the time of Charles I. And you only had to go back one more stage before then, and you were back in the age of Queen Elizabeth I, Drake, Raleigh and Shakespeare.

73

While he was musing on this, Mr Pope had gone off to fetch some weights for the old-fashioned scales, leaving Colin to wander about the farmyard. There was a barn, with the doors wide open, and a small quantity of hay inside. Colin entered and looked around. There was not much hay left, but perhaps it would not be long before the farm could be gathering more to restock the barn for the winter. He went further inside, and seeing some hay lying loose on the floor of the barn decided to try his hand with the pitchfork which he noticed standing up against the wooden wall. He practised with the amount on the ground, throwing it up on to the heap, and it dropped down again. He pushed the fork forward to lift it again, and this time the prongs went well into the pile of hay. It was not such a simple operation after all. Furthermore, he had struck something hard with one of the prongs, so he thought he had better inspect to see if he had done any damage.

He scraped some of the hay away and felt inside with his fingers. At once a little fall of hay revealed that it had been covering a wooden barrel about two feet tall, and this was what the fork had hit. The barrel seemed intact, and when he tried to move it, quite clearly it was full and he could feel a liquid swilling around inside it when he rocked it. Now why should a barrel be underneath a pile of hay? The liquid could not be for farm use, because if it was fuel oil, say, it would not be left where it could set alight the entire barn. And why a barrel and not a metal container?

Then it suddenly occurred to him what it must be, and he threw the hay back over it as fast as he was able, glancing rapidly over his shoulder several times in case Mr Pope should return. It could not be anything but brandy, which was distilled in France and was very expensive—if Customs duty were paid on it. He had seen bottles of brandy in the wine shop near where he lived, and the most expensive had astonished him by being priced at nearly seven pounds a bottle. Even a barrel that size—the likely cost in a shop of the number of bottles which could be filled from it frightened him, and he redoubled his efforts, to return to the sunlight just in time for Mr Pope to appear with a couple of heavy weights in his hands, ready to weigh the potatoes for his great-aunt. And there had been three boat-loads!

'Here y'are, then,' said Mr Pope, pointing to a sack on the ground. 'You'll manage to carry that all right with no trouble.'

Colin handed him the five pound note and Mr Pope gave him the change, slowly, from money in his pocket, and Colin swung the sack over his shoulder and left as casually as he dared under the circumstances.

So it seemed that Fred's uncle was one of those behind it all. But he could not be the only one. There was Mr Trewan, who according to Derek owned the boat. There were the two men on the boat which took trippers round the bay. There were the secret meetings of the boys in the village. Now Colin could see another reason why there were no girls at those meetings. The biggest of them had to be strong enough to row a heavy boat, and girls might not be strong enough. Also, like him, the boys from the village must hold the prejudice which no Sex Discrimination Act could disperse, that girls could not be trusted with secrets.

On the other hand—suppose that the hidden barrel was not really hidden at all, but just kept there because that was where Mr Pope always kept that barrel for some reason best known to himself. Or even there was the possibility that somebody else was hiding it there and the farmer knew nothing about it. It could even be that it was not brandy, or if it was that it had not been smuggled.

It was very confusing. He had heard tales of Cornish wreckers, who used to lure ships on to the rocks with false lights so that they could be robbed. He had also heard tales of Cornish smugglers, but both kinds of stories, although for the most part true, concerned a period long gone, not modern times.

'It took you long enough,' declared Aunt Daphne as he walked in through her cottage door. 'Don't put it down there, put the sack outside in the shed. We don't want soil on the carpet. I suppose he was as slow and talkative as he always was. What did he talk to you about?'

Colin grinned. 'He said if he didn't hurry up you'd be after him.'

He slipped out as soon as he was able, and made for the cove. He had something to find out. In the village he came across Simon, who apart from having one arm strapped up seemed happy enough now. Colin greeted him.

'How's the arm?' he asked.

'Okay now.'

'You shouldn't have dived.'

As he made the remark Colin realized that it was a foolish statement. If he had not dived, he would most likely have been thrown in—or worse—but even without that possibility. the boy had had to dive or to face what amounted to a life-time of humiliation for as long as he should live in that village.

'Perhaps you had no choice, though,' he concluded lamely. 'Hard luck.'

'My own fault. It'll be all right in a few weeks, a month or so,' said the boy seriously. 'Going down to the beach?'

'If you like,' said Colin easily.

'Come with you if you like.'

They set off together, and after they had arrived Colin made a point of edging the two of them towards the cave where the boat was kept. The tide was low. Inside the cave the dinghy was still covered by its tarpaulin, and Colin could tell that the outboard had been removed. There was not a sign of any of its cargo from the previous period of darkness.

'What are you looking for?' asked Simon curiously.

'Oh, nothing. Just looking around. Have you ever been out in it?'

Simon shook his head.

'I have. Derek took me in it once. I haven't been in it when the outboard was fitted, though. Do they use the outboard very often?'

He was given a side-long glance. 'On special occasions they use it,' the boy said.

'Like last night?' pumped Colin.

'I don't know. Did anyone use the boat last night?'

'I think so.'

'Oh. I'll have to go now,' said Simon suddenly, 'because I mustn't be late back. Are you going to stay on the beach for a while?'

Colin said that he would return later, and Simon left, with Colin thinking that he was a very odd character indeed who deserved to have had his collar-bone broken. He had not been actually unfriendly, but for sure he was not someone with whom you could easily make friends. He had time to make his way back for lunch via the road which led down to the café, rather than take the short route along the cliff, and he left the beach fairly soon after the other boy had departed. As he was ascending the café platform he happened to notice the boy with the broken collar bone just at the top of the cliff and walking along the path.

That, he thought, was odd, for Simon had been gone for long enough to be half-way to his home by then, not still to be visible from the beach. He thought nothing more of it, however, assuming that the other had paused for some reason, perhaps to greet a friend on the beach, and set off up the road which led out of the beach car park.

The road was a long way round, there was no doubt about it. Part-way along, Colin could see in the near distance the tower of the village church, yet to get there by this route would take ages. He stopped, and wondered. There were two grassy fields between him and the village crossroads, he judged, divided by a hedge. If he could cut across these—or more sensibly walk round the edges of them so as not to tread down the crops of grass—he would save no end of time. He found a gate, swung over it with a gate-vault such as he had been taught at school, and set off.

There was a gap in the hedge, which he passed through, where grass did not grow. By the appearance of it, this was a regular route for somebody. On the other side grew a clump of trees and he could see his way before him. The trees grew in a group, almost like an oasis, with rough ground in the centre and vegetation growing high. In the very centre appeared to be some kind of hole, such as one a very large wild animal might make. Perhaps it was a badger's set. He had never seen a badger's set, so he stepped forward to investigate, but even though he had never seen a badger, either, he would have been very surprised if these animals were large enough to have made a hole of that kind. For one thing, the hole was too wide at the top, and for another it descended almost vertically for a few feet on to a small stretch of level soil and where it went then he could not tell because of overhanging vegetation. He thought that maybe it went nowhere, and that what he could see was the whole of it.

Still, he had saved time by not walking the long way round, so he could spend a minute in this hole, and lowered himself in. He trod on some nettles, slid violently on to his bottom, and found instead of resistance to his feet which he outstretched to stop himself—nothing but empty space!

EIGHT

THE BOYS TURN NASTY

When he found himself falling, sliding forward on his back into some kind of void, Colin's immediate thought was that he was about to drop down the shaft of a derelict tin mine. If this was what he was doing, the chances of survival were slight. In the first place, the fall alone would probably kill him, and even if it did not he would lie injured at the bottom of the shaft for days until he died of starvation, for nobody would have any inkling of where he was.

He grabbed hold of everything he could find in order to stop his fall, and in the process stung his hands badly on a bunch of tall nettles, but despite the pain he clung on. To his great relief the nettles were rooted firmly in the ground, and his forward movement stopped. He hung, with his legs to beyond half-way up his thighs, down the hole. This was never a badger's set, that was for certain. As long as he lay still, he was safe, so he lay motionless on his back and thought the matter out logically.

More than half of him was on ground which did not slope too sleeply. Had he not trodden on something slippery he would not have fallen at all. So it was the thought of the drop which was terrifying, not his present position. For the present, in fact, he was perfectly safe. All he had to do was draw himself out without moving further forward. Suppose there was not a drop at all, then how would he extricate himself?

Considering the matter that way, the answer was simple.

He would sit up, shuffle back a little, and then just stand upright and get out. If he did not panic, there would be no problem at all. So the first thing was to lower his legs carefully. and wriggle backwards.

When he sat up he found he was sitting on a broad stone, with just below head-height and facing him another stone just as big and looking like a kind of supporting beam. It disappeared into the undergrowth on either side of him. Well, that would not give way in a hurry and neither, now he noticed them, would the two vertical stones which were set on either side to form a kind of stonework frame about a yard square. He pressed his still-stinging hands firmly on either side of the opening to ensure that he would not fall, and out of curiosity peered inside to see if he could find any clue as to the depth of the shaft.

As his eyes grew accustomed to the dim interior, he began to feel rather a fool. It was not a shaft at all. He could see an earthen floor just a few feet below him, with a passage several feet wide running away on either side. He might have twisted an ankle had he fallen into this unexpectedly, but as it was he was in no danger whatever. He turned round and lowered himself inside.

The passage was low, not tall enough for him to stand upright. Over him was a roof of solid rock. This was what he had taken to be a beam running across. On both sides the walls were lined with vertical pillars of rock. The opening through which he had just passed had quite obviously been made deliberately. Certainly, this was nothing to do with a tin mine.

He took a few paces to the right, but the light was dim because of the small entrance hole. He traversed the entrance and tried the other side, and that was just as dark. Well, he was not going to risk exploring further without a light, just in case. He scrambled out, determined to return shortly to investigate more of this.

After he had eaten and performed his after-meal chores,

he went by himself to the holiday cottage where he and his mother slept. He knew they had brought two electric torches with them.

'We don't know what this country cottage is going to be like,' his mother had said before they had left home. 'I haven't seen this aunt of mine for years, and for all I know we can expect to find some ruin of a house lit only by candles. So we'd better take torches with us, just in case.'

He remembered that he had been excited at the time by the idea of spending a full month on holiday near the sea, but a little apprehensive firstly about meeting a possibly permanently-complaining, nagging great-aunt and secondly about having to stay in what might have turned out to have been a crumbling hovel. He was glad that neither of those had been the case—far from it, in both instances.

This time he descended the hole more carefully, only partly because of the nettle-rash on his hands, and stepped confidently into the underground passage, switched on the torch and headed to the right of the entrance. So far, all seemed well. He kept the ground well-lit, just in case it should suddenly disappear from in front of him, but the earth remained firm and the roof remained at the same level throughout.

Before long the passage branched off in two directions, like a T-junction on a road. Turning right, he found that he was inside a small chamber which was a dead end, so he turned back and tried going to the left. This, too, came to a dead end, but before it did, laid on end in a row before the wall of stone, he saw four barrels, exactly similar to the one he had found under the hay.

In some confusion he walked back, crouching somewhat because of the lowness of the roof, and tried the far side of the entrance. There the design was repeated—the passage led to two more equally-sized, slightly elongated chambers, and against the wall of one four barrels stood on end. This, then, was where they had been placed for safe keeping. He shook one of the barrels and heard and felt liquid swill around inside. He wished that he had a penknife, so that he could make a hole in the top of one just to check.

Three trips in the dinghy had been made between the boats. He now saw the reason for the outboard motor. With a boat full of barrels an engine would move the boat faster than rowing could. He estimated that each trip could carry say six barrels. That meant eighteen barrels could have been brought ashore, or maybe just a few less. Here were eight; one at the farm made nine. Where were the rest? Who had them?

His first thought now was to contact the police. He would be able to telephone from the village easily enough. But if he did, when the police arrived they would first want to talk to him and soon everybody would know what he had been doing.

He emerged from the entrance to the secret underground passage complex and walked away quickly round the edge of the field, for he did not want to be found too near to the evidence, so to speak. When he reached the road, he paused and leaned against the gate while he thought some more. He realized that he still had the torch in his hand, so he stuffed it into the pocket of his jeans where it would not be seen.

If he told the police, he could tell them about stowing away in the dinghy, and about the boat in the harbour, and about the hidden barrels of what must be contraband. That meant Mark would be in trouble, and the two men who ran the boat, and Fred's uncle at the farm—and all the boys in the village. And that was just for a start. He didn't know where it would end, because he had no way of telling just who was really involved in the business. There was Mr Trewan, for instance, and of course Derek.

No, it wouldn't do. The police would take the barrels as evidence of some kind, but that would not mean anything. There was no proof he could possible produce, only point a nasty finger of suspicion which would cause him to lead a most miserable existence for the rest of his stay in the village, and that might spread to include Aunt Daphne and his mother as well. He knew quite well that if he did call the police the village boys would not let him get away with it.

The dilemma was a most difficult one for someone as basically law-abiding as himself. He was also loyal to his friends, however, even new-found ones. You don't tell tales when it is nothing to do with yourself and nobody is getting hurt. It was not as if it was even a robbery taking place. No one was being robbed, except the Government. But then again, was a bank robbery any the less a crime because it was not an individual being stolen from but a large organization? The answer clearly was that it was a very serious crime. But smuggling was almost a game. Their next-door neighbours at home had told his mother with pride how they had smuggled a wrist watch into the country when they had returned from their holiday abroad.

Nevertheless, it was far more than a game when it occurred on such a large scale as this, it was more of a business designed to make a great deal of money for someone. It was also more than a game when it was taken so seriously by Derek and the others, that they would injure other boys deliberately if they talked about it. No—there was something nasty about it—and something deadly, as his encounter with the artist and all the elaborate precautions at the studio demonstrated.

He found Fred watching him.

'Thought you'd gone into a trance,' said Fred, 'the way you were looking into space.'

'I was thinking,' explained Colin.

'So that's how you look,' said Fred unkindly. 'So I haven't seen you think before. What were you thinking about?'

'I've found a queer underground passage,' said Colin in a burst of confidence. 'It's over there, in that clump of trees between the two fields.'

'Oh yes?' Fred did not seem over-enthusiastic.

'Yes. It's most unusual, sort of low, and as if it's been

there for centuries. There's a kind of chamber at each end.'

'Coming swimming tonight?' asked Fred. 'There'll be a meeting, because the tide's right.'

'Okay.'

'I'll call for you, then,' said Fred. 'I've got things to do just now for my uncle.'

Fred had not been wearing a shirt again, and his tanned body reminded Colin that he had not had much luck in obtaining a tan for himself. He had turned red in places, but there was not a trace of real brown at all. It must be something to do with the colour of his hair, he thought sadly. It was disappointing. It was odd that Fred had shown so little interest in his exciting find.

He and Fred arrived early at the beach, and spent nearly an hour in the water before Derek and Mark made their appearance. By then, most of the holidaymakers had departed and the small crowd of boys were ringing the amphitheatre round the pool. One of the rituals seemed to be that no boy should dry himself, but should sit or crouch dripping on the black rocks. It must be a demonstration of their hardiness, or something.

Expectant silence fell as Derek made his entry and performed his ceremonial dive, swam to the side and climbed out. It was a clear demonstration of who was the leader. Then he stood at the pinnacle and several others dived in turn, showing their prowess too.

'Ginger,' called Derek, 'you going to dive?'

Colin nodded, made his ascent to the top, and as he stood on the ledge found that this time the experience felt almost commonplace. When he began to swim to the side he noticed that all of the others were leaving the rock pile and were forming a group at the lower end of the pool.

'Is that it for tonight, then?' he said as he walked out, shaking the water from his eyes and ears.

Derek stepped forward, until he was standing in front of Colin. There were no visitors remaining, now. Colin surveyed the assembled boys before him. Simon was not among them, but of course there was no point in his being there, and he also observed that Fred was well to the rear.

'What's going on?' asked Colin, walking forward on to the sand.

'People don't talk,' said Derek. Then he hit him with a power-driver in the centre of the chest, strong enough to stagger Colin several paces back.

'What was that for?' demanded Colin wrathfully.

'They don't pry into what doesn't concern them, either,' added Derek, hitting him again, 'or they regret it.'

'Get lost,' said Colin. 'What are you talking about?'

Then Derek stepped back at the same instant as Colin, smaller though he was, was squaring up to him partly in bewilderment but mainly in a great, consuming rage. As Derek moved back the crowd of boys surged in simultaneously and attacked, not singly but all at once and Colin was driven back to the rock face, where he fell over backwards under the combined onslaught and where they continued to hit him ferociously and savagely.

He fought back fiercely, landing blows as hard as he was able on every portion of every available naked body within striking distance. One boy staggered back with blood dribbling from a cut lip; another reeled from a blow delivered from a hard-clenched fist which had landed just behind his right eye. He found that they were not fighting according to any rules, and felt fingers digging into him, nipping him savagely, clawing at him like animals, in addition to the blows which were pouring down upon him like iron hail stones. He also noticed one fact which surprised him at the time, which was that none of them was punching him in the face, as if they did not wish to leave any visible marks.

Certainly he was losing. He could not move out of the way, pinned down as he was under the weight of bodies, and the pain from the multitude of blows was growing more intense. Finally he felt his legs being pulled apart by cruel hands, and then he doubled up in agony as the final punch landed between them. He felt sick immediately. Then they left him alone, at some signal which he was not in a position to see, and all drew back.

'You were warned,' announced Mark with evil in his voice, coming into vision, 'that nobody talks. Now are you going to talk again—to anyone?'

The rest of the boys were wandering away as if nothing had happened, although the one with the cut lip was trying to stem the flow of blood and another was rubbing the side of his temple. Derek had gone. Colin could just notice this through the tears which he could not blink away. He was still moaning a little, but hearing himself as if from a distance he stopped immediately and lay in writhing silence.

'That was your punishment, and it was a mild one. Promise to keep your tongue to yourself, and that will be the end of it. If not—'

Colin nodded, and was left alone. The pain was passing. He sat up slowly and saw that his body was a mass of red marks, which would probably become bruises by the morning. He felt stiff. He breathed deeply three times, and still did not understand what it was that he was supposed to have said. He had only talked to Fred, about the passage, and . . .

So that was it. Fred! That was why he had not been interested in the passage. He had turned out to be a traitor, telling Derek that Colin had discovered the secret passage—and that was talking out of turn, to this lot. So they did know about the barrels down there. It was all part of their 'activities'. He felt miserable. Then he saw Fred standing over him, carrying his clothes for him.

'You rotten creep!' said Colin through clenched teeth. 'You told them that I'd talked to you. You'll never be spoken to by me again, so don't pretend to be a friend of mine. Clear off!'

Fred looked at him solemnly. 'You didn't tell me anything that I told anyone else about,' he said, quietly. 'I know who

86

you did talk to, though. Who was it, do you think, who would want to creep back into Derek's favour after what happened to him?'

'You mean you knew they were going to do this to me, and didn't warn me?' Colin was hurt and baffled.

'I didn't know till I got down here tonight. And what could I do then?' Fred shrugged. 'It's all right, though. It won't make any difference. Once somebody's been given a punishment, we none of us remember it afterwards. Simon was stupid. He didn't realize that.'

So that was why Simon had taken so long to reach the path on his way up from the beach! After Colin had talked to him in the cave, foolishly trying to pump information out of him, he would have gone straight to the café and reported him to the leader of the boys, probably making more of it than had actually been said. Simon would have made a good Nazi informer. And Mark, for all his pleasant face when he smiled, could be envisaged as the one who would have been in charge of a Gestapo unit, because there was little doubt that he had enjoyed leading the punishment attack. The others—well, they did as they were told, which also explained a great deal of how a group of normally decent people could be controlled and manipulated.

Fred held out a hand and helped Colin to his feet, then offered Colin the towel so that he could dry himself and wipe away the sand in which he had rolled during the fight. 'I didn't hit you,' he said.

'You didn't do anything to stop them.'

'Don't be silly. What good would that have done? It's over now, anyway. You won't hear any more about it. And in a way you did break the most important rule.'

Regretfully, Colin had to admit to himself that he had. Even while he was thinking this, he also realized that he was in fact condoning that he deserved to have been punished, just as if any of the gang should be punished. It also struck him at the same time that the chief rule in reality was the belief that Derek Trewan knew best and should be obeyed. At that, he remained silent.

'Coming?' asked Fred kindly when Colin was dressed.

'No—you go on. I'll walk slowly. I don't feel like being with anyone at the moment. Thanks, though,' he added gratefully. Fred understood and scampered off, knowing now that Colin bore him no grudge.

At the place where the path led into the road, he decided that he had to walk a little more to calm down before he could go home to face his mother and Aunt Daphne, and set off with the intention of going to the harbour and back. Most of the way was in darkness, and no one would see him and he could be alone. It startled him to hear his name spoken as he passed the studio. The artist was standing in the shadows outside.

'Taking an evening constitutional, Colin?'

'Oh. I didn't see you. Just thought I'd have a walk down,' he replied.

'Come in, if you like.'

The studio was lighted, and no paintings had been sold since there were no gaps round the walls where the pictures had been spaced evenly. On the easel the landscape with the cottage was uncovered, with a final touch of wet paint still glistening. The artist closed the door, but did not lock it.

'Been down to the beach?' the man asked. Colin nodded. 'I hope you dried your back well after swimming, or later on you could develop rheumatism in your dorsal muscles.' He laid a hand on Colin's back, as if feeling if it was wet, and Colin winced involuntarily.

Immediately the man flicked up Colin's shirt and examined his bare back rapidly, then in the same movement his chest, dropping the shirt again quickly after he had done so. 'Going to tell me?' he enquired. 'Who's beaten you up?'

'Nobody. Fell on some rocks.'

'Back and front? How unusual!' the man drawled.

'Just some rocks,' repeated Colin firmly.

'Somebody found out you knew too much, and afraid you might talk?' persisted the man, seating himself on a stool near one of the tables and looking the boy full in the face searchingly.

Colin shrugged. He could see no reason why he should tell this stranger anything. There was a long silence.

'Well then,' continued the man eventually, 'let's say that if somebody thought you had spoken out of turn, that somebody would want to make sure that you knew that you mustn't do it again. So he'd want to impress you with the importance of not talking, with what you might call a foretaste of what might happen if you did it again. So at one of your meetings on the beach, that somebody would arrange that your—shall we say?—error was drawn to your attention in a way you wouldn't forget.'

He paused again, and Colin still said nothing.

'Now if I had been the one who had been impressed in that way, I would think that my best plan would be to take notice of the warning—and to keep my nose clean in future. Wouldn't you agree that might be the best plan?'

'Yeah, most likely, if that's what happened,' agreed Colin cautiously.

'So I would say you ought to keep quiet about it all, at any rate for the time being. And I should be a bit cautious when I got to my home town, in case that somebody had any friends there who got to hear that you'd been talking.'

That was reminiscent of earlier advice, and it did not sound very friendly. Colin was a little worried. Yet this man had looked after him so carefully after he had stowed away in the dinghy. The artist smiled as if reading his thoughts in his face.

'Cheer up. You won't come to any harm through me, I can promise you that. Do what you have to, but keep out of trouble as far as you can and you'll be all right. Oh, by the way, I wouldn't let your mother or Mrs Johnson see those marks if you can avoid it. If they do, make them think you slipped on a rock, eh?' Then he was apparently deadly serious as he added: 'But if there's any real trouble, come straight here, using the key, and don't hesitate.'

The artist did not know what had happened, then, or was guessing pretty accurately. He decided to take his advice. As he slipped out through the door to go home, Colin thought that he noticed a figure in the shadows, further down the road, but could not be sure.

NINE

THE SEA TRIP

The weather was holding beautifully. Every day was dawning as brightly as the previous one, with barely a cloud in the blue sky but tiny, white fluffy ones very high up. It was a glorious summer. In the local weekly newspaper he read a letter from an irate resident that the watering of smallholding and farms was forbidden so that there would be sufficient water for the tourists to have baths, and asking which was the more important, tourists' baths or the production of food.

It was a surprise to him, therefore, when his mother told him over breakfast that she wanted him to dress properly that morning.

'Where are we going?' he asked.

'Church,' was the brief reply. 'It's Sunday.'

'You needn't be too dressed up,' put in Aunt Daphne, almost as an admonishment to his mother, 'because the vicar is quite happy for people to turn up in their holiday clothes, if they're visitors.'

'I'm a resident,' declared Colin. After what had happened, he felt like one. He argued intuitively that had he been merely a visitor, the local boys would not have dared to have invited him to join them, nor have given him a severe beating. It was like logic turned on its head, that because he was accepted as one of them he had got hurt, whereas if he had been a tourist he would not have been, but it was true.

'Then residents do dress for church,' said his great-aunt, smiling with shrewd approval. 'They make a proper job of it. You need to be there for half-past ten. We shall set out earlier because of this blamed leg.'

It was a short but slow walk to the church, for every person in the village who was attending that morning seemed to pause to talk with Aunt Daphne. Sometimes she would stop walking entirely, resting on her stick—for she had discarded the crutches for this event.

It was not a large congregation, and many of them were women, with just a handful of strangers in almost-holiday clothes mingled with them. The vicar, a grey-haired man with a ruddy face, greeted them at the door, and there was another short gossip with him before Aunt Daphne led Colin and his mother down the aisle to the front pew on the left, where she sat down firmly, her leg stretched straight before her almost defiantly, and her walking-stick propped against the dark brown of the seat. She reminded Colin just a little of photographs he had seen of Queen Victoria, and then to complete the image she turned her head to survey the other pews nearby and incline her head at intervals to friends and subjects. In each case, a respectful smile and nod was returned.

Colin half-turned as all but Aunt Daphne stood for the choir to process up the church. Near the back of the church he noticed the artist, who saw Colin glancing at him but who did not acknowledge in any way that he recognized him.

The service began. The choir consisted exclusively of the boys whom he knew, and when it was their turn to sing they did so beautifully. Their naturally tanned faces were all that prevented a deceptively angelic appearance on the part of each of them with their neatly-brushed hair, scrubbed skins and shining white surplices, and at the end of the service Derek left his place with a subdued gait, held aloft the large, ornately-carved brass cross, and the choir, followed by the vicar, filed out in pairs behind him while the organ played.

Colin and his family were the last out of the church, and while Aunt Daphne was greeted for a second time by the vicar, who talked to her for a very long time, involving his mother and himself in the conversation as well, the choir boys now in their ordinary clothes passed from time to time into the open air. Colin lost interest after a while and went outside to wait in the sunshine.

The artist was visible near the churchyard gate, but as Colin emerged from the church porch he glanced at him and without a sign of recognition immediately set off down the road. That, thought Colin, was certainly odd. He had expected at least a surreptitious nod in his direction, but it was as if Colin had suddenly become invisible.

At the gate, in the shade of an overhanging tree, Derek was talking to Mark, then he walked off by himself while Mark came back inside the churchyard a few paces and spoke a few words to one of the younger boys, before himself walking away. The younger boy, all smiles—but Colin recalled that even he had been taking part in the attack upon him the previous evening—ran back towards the church door and touched Colin nervously on the elbow to attract his attention.

'I've been told to tell you that it's your turn tonight,' said the boy, very quietly in his ear.

'What do I have to do?'

'I was told to tell you to ask Fred if you didn't know,' the smaller boy replied, then hurried off to join some of the others who were playing leap-frog over the tombstones, until the disapproving gazes of some of the older members of the congregation drove them away.

When he did find Fred, shortly before his mother and Aunt Daphne ended their conversation and came slowly out, it was round the back of the church, where in an empty space he and a group of the choir were playing football with a tennis ball. Colin drew him on one side. He asked him. Fred took him to a buttress where they could not be seen by any but the rest of the boys.

'It means you're to take the dinghy out. You have to be at the cave where the boat is about half-past eight.'

'Then what?' asked Colin, pretending that he had no idea, just to be on the safe side.

'You'll be told when you get there. But what you do is row the boat out a little way, then you get picked up by another boat, then you go for a short trip in her, then they bring you back and you row to the shore again. And that's it. It's dead easy.'

'But what do I have to do it for?'

Fred's face instantly assumed a cagey look, and Colin was reminded that when he had asked Fred before about the boat trip he had said that he had not wanted to get him too involved. Well, now he was being told to become involved.

'There are reasons,' he said.

'That's just what you said when I asked you why you were going, when you were picked—remember?'

Fred dropped his mask and pulled Colin further into the corner where they could not be overheard by anyone. 'Look, Colin,' he said, glancing round nervously, 'I've got to live here all the time, but in a few weeks you'll be gone. It's best you don't know some things, then you can't get into trouble, because I wouldn't like that.' He was speaking with difficulty over the choice of words, or so it seemed, because his naturally slow speech became even hesitant in places, almost as if begging Colin not to want more information from him.

Colin heard his mother calling his name. 'Come swimming this afternoon?' Fred invited suddenly.

'Okay. Where'll I see you?'

'Call for me. Two houses past the general store.'

'Okay.' Then Colin ran off to join his mother and her aunt, to walk sedately with them back to the house.

'Duty done,' said his great-aunt with satisfaction, unpinning her hat and sinking thankfully into her armchair. 'But I think I'll return to the crutches next time I go out. That stick takes a bit out of me, and I was wrong to be too proud.'

While Colin's mother hung up her hat for her, on the peg

94

at the back of the door, Colin himself tried to test how much the old lady really knew of what went on in the village.

'Aunt Daphne,' he said, 'do you know there's a sort of underground passage in the village?'

She looked at him thoughtfully.

'Oh yes?' she said with a trace of suspicion in her tone of voice. 'Who told you?'

'I found it. I almost fell down it. What's it for?'

'Ah, yes.' The old lady hesitated a little. 'It's a very old passage, very old indeed.'

'But what is it for?'

She laughed. 'Goodness me, does everything have to be *for* something? It's not for anything now, but years ago it might have been for almost anything—to hide in, perhaps.'

'To hide what in?'

'Who knows? Possibly people, hiding from marauders or their enemies.'

'But who knows it's there?'

'Why, everybody in the village I should think, but we don't talk about it, or else we'd have archaeologists arriving in droves, and the Ministry of Works putting up signs, and the place would be swarming with visitors all buying tickets to have a look down it, like at Stonehenge.'

'It's as old as Stonehenge?'

'Most likely even older, but when it was found, years ago, there was a kind of agreement that nobody would be told because we didn't want the village itself to become a tourist attraction, or the farming would suffer. So everybody kept quiet about it, and I think you ought to, as well.'

And that was all Colin could extract in the way of information, because thereafter Aunt Daphne shut up like a clam despite Colin's efforts to draw her out. At length all she would add was that she would tell him all she knew about it before he went home. So it seemed that Aunt Daphne, at any rate, knew nothing about hidden barrels, but with that Colin had to be satisfied for the time being.

Fred's house was an ordinary cottage on the main road, road, and when he knocked at the door that afternoon Fred himself answered and came out at once. He tried to gather more from Fred about what might be expected that evening, but Fred, too, would not be drawn any more, and he thought it best not to reveal what he knew about the hidden passage, so the two of them spent the afternoon innocuously and innocently swimming in the sea and playing on the beach or climbing the hot rocks in the sun.

In the evening, Colin found a suitable excuse to leave the house and when it was growing dark was to be discovered down in the cave, dressed warmly in case the breeze at sea should make him feel chilly. The cave was deserted, so he passed the time by removing the tarpaulin and folding it as neatly as he was able. Then he thought. It had better not be believed that he knew what was expected, or someone might grow uncomfortably suspicious, so after he had folded the canvas he laid it on the dry sand rather than in the bows of the boat. Then Derek arrived, silently.

'Hello, Ginger,' he greeted softly.

Colin turned, startled. 'Where'm I supposed to row this thing?' he demanded. 'And why me, anyway?'

'Because, Ginger, you can row. And once you've taken part you'll be less inclined to speak out of turn, won't you, because then you'll really have become one of us. Not like that Simon idiot. He won't be able to join in properly for a year or two yet. He's what you might call—padding—like the rest of the younger ones.' Derek spoke with contempt. 'Now, don't leave that cover on the sand, you put it inside the boat. Here. Help me stuff it up this end.'

They pushed the canvas into the bows.

'So what do I do?' Colin tried to make himself sound just a little eager to set off on the adventure.

Derek glanced at a wristwatch, tilting it a little so the light would strike it more clearly.

'In exactly ten minutes from now, we shall push the boat

into the water, then you will row straight out to sea—over in that direction,' he said, pointing.

'What if it's rough out there?'

'It isn't. Then after you've been rowing for perhaps another ten minutes or so, a boat will turn up. You know that boat in the harbour, the big one?'

Colin nodded.

'Well, that. Row towards it, and it'll stop. You'll get on board quite easily, then when you're on the boat, just stay there until it brings you back again, when you get into the dinghy and row back here, because they'll tow this boat behind them so you can do that. Have a fag?'

He proffered a packet of cigarettes, and Colin shook his head.

'Oh no, you're a goody-goody, aren't you? I forgot.' Colin did not see what was supposed to be so goody-goody about not smoking, and his opinion of Derek sank yet another notch lower down the scale. Derek puffed regularly, sitting inside the boat, while Colin watched him, until he suddenly looked at his watch again, jumped up and said it was time.

They dragged the boat across the sand until it was just afloat. Colin stepped in. Derek instructed him to take an oar and give a good shove off with it over the stern.

'How will I know exactly where the cove is when I come back in the dark?'

'I'll wave a flashlight every now and then when I judge it's time. Then just head towards the light. You can't go wrong.'

Then Colin was on his own, and rowing steadily out to sea. There was a feeling of isolation, all by himself with only the slap-slap of waves against the boat for company. It was still light enough for him to discern the coastline, but on the beach was nobody at all. Derek had disappeared. When he turned his head to check that he was rowing in the right direction, there was nothing at all. The sun had descended below the rim of the horizon, and he could not tell where the sea ended and the sky began. As waves grew a little higher and the boat rocked more than in the shelter of the cove, he began to worry about what to do if he capsized should an extra-powerful wave hit the boat broadside. The rowing was becoming a little more difficult to control, especially as he was not used to it, and he did not like the way in which the coast was now so far distant, farther than he thought he could possibly swim if the worse came to the worst.

Colin rested on his oars for a moment, because his nose had begun to itch, and found that at once he was being carried off course. There was a little wind, too, now, and he was glad that he had had the forethought to dress warmly.

Then he heard it, from somewhere over to his right but still in the distance—a throbbing of an engine. Before many more minutes had passed he could just distinguish the low outline of the boat from Geraint's Cove harbour moving steadily in his direction. The navigation lights were on. He kept rowing straight before him, for if he had not he would have been swept back towards the coast, then very quickly it seemed the boat was heading directly towards him and he stopped rowing, and as he did so the boat slowed down. He could make out little flashes of white at the bows as the water was raised into small, frothy waves. Then the engine dropped to tick-over speed, and a wooden step-ladder was hooked over the side by one of the two figures on board. He rowed towards it with short, powerful strokes and stood up precariously to hold out the painter of the dinghy. This was taken by the man who had lowered the ladder, who also held out a hand to help him on board.

Nobody said a word, but the same man dragged the dinghy round to the stern and tied it securely. At the wheel, under a weather shelter which extended for not more than a quarter of the distance to the back of the boat, a man with a pipe stood watching the operation, and when it was complete he opened the throttle by pushing forward a small lever, and the boat headed farther out towards the open sea.

Colin remained where he had climbed into the boat, and after perhaps a minute the one who had helped him up came along and lifted on board again the steps from the side, placing them underneath the seat which ran all the way round the inside of the boat then joining the man with the pipe. Still neither of the men spoke, so Colin walked forward underneath the cover which acted as a wheelhouse and peered out into the dimness ahead.

'So you're Colin,' said the man with the pipe at last, not taking his eyes from the water ahead. He was not asking a question but making a statement of fact. No doubt Derek— or someone—had given him the information. 'If you want a lavatory, there's one in the forepeak.' He removed the pipe from his mouth and used it to point towards a varnished door down two steps in front of them. 'We have every comfort for our passengers.'

The other man chuckled. 'Have some chocolate,' he urged, handing a complete bar to Colin, who accepted it gratefully.

The two of them were dressed in thick, dark jerseys, and on their feet they wore what Colin took to be seaboots. They looked typical fisherman, Colin thought.

'Where are we going?' he asked after a minute or two.

'Oh, just a pleasure cruise,' said the one who had given him the chocolate. 'Were you a bit scared when you rowed out?'

'Just a bit,' Colin admitted.

'Thought we might be wanting to feed you to the fishes?'

'No. Hadn't been out that far to sea in a rowing boat before.'

'Ah. You were safe enough.'

It grew darker. The helmsman flicked on a light and by its glow inspected his watch. Then he knocked the throttle lever further forward and the boat picked up speed. They were certainly not following the line of the coast, but heading straight out. A minute or two later, and the helmsman switched off the navigation lights and did not turn them on

99

again. Colin wondered what would happen if there was another boat in the vicinity which would not now be able to see them, and what he ought to do if there was a crash. He peered out of the side windows, but could see nothing but the water, so as casually as he could he strolled back down the boat. Even without the glass in the way, he could see no better. They might just as well have been alone in the world. Behind, the dinghy was bobbing its way through the waves. He returned to the shelter of the wheelhouse.

'Cup o'tea?' enquired the man who had given him the chocolate, and poured some out of a huge flask and handed him the cup. It was hot and sweet. The boat lurched a little, and he spilt some, so he took out his handkerchief to wipe it off his trousers.

'Not got your sea legs yet, eh?' said the man. They both seemed pleasant enough, and Colin could not make out at all where they were going, or why they were going there. If they were expecting to meet another ship, they did not appear to be making any kind of preparation. It struck him as odd. He had been expecting to have to be in the company of what he might have called hard villains, and yet here he was being treated as if a pleasure outing had been arranged just for his benefit.

'Beyond the limit yet, do you reckon?' grunted the man with the pipe, some while later.

'Easily,' said the other.

'Right then.' He closed the throttle, and the boat rolled as if aimlessly for the next few minutes until Colin thought that he might soon be feeling sick. Then: 'That'll about do.' And since his pipe had gone out, the man who had been smoking it tapped it on the heel of his boot, felt the bowl with the palm of his hand, and slipped it firmly into his pocket. Then the engine picked up, the boat turned and headed back the way it had come.

Colin asked if that was all there was to it.

'Aye, that's all for tonight.'

'But we haven't done anything.'

'What did you want—a firework display?'

The other man chuckled again. Colin could not see any point in it. He had not exactly expected that they would have taken on board a load of barrels, because if they had intended to do that the dinghy would have been fitted with the outboard motor, but at least he had supposed there would have been some sort of action. As it was, nothing had happened at all—they had just gone out to sea, and then begun to return. That reference to *the limit* he thought he understood easily— they had crossed the limit of territorial waters, so they had technically left the boundaries of England and had been on the high seas, where British law could not be enforced—but what its significance was that night he had no idea at all.

'Dummy run tonight,' said the man who had been smoking the pipe, as if reading his thoughts. 'Throws them off the scent.'

So that was the reason! By now it was pitch black. Still the navigation lights had not been switched on, either because there was still some reason or simply because the helmsman had forgotten. He was about to risk asking why this was when suddenly from not far away another boat, larger than this and moving very fast, turned on not only navigation lights, red, green, and at the top of a short mast white, but a powerful searchlight as well. It swept towards their boat and as it did so another searchlight came on to illuminate them from one end to the other.

'Heave to!' came a loud instruction through a loudspeaker. 'Her Majesty's Customs and Excise. Identify yourself!'

The coastguard cutter moved in until it was standing off not more than the length of a swimming bath away, keeping its searchlights firmly on the smaller craft. The friendlier of the two men glanced at the other and smiled. The one at the wheel stopped the engine and called from the centre of the boat.

'What do you want?'

'Identify yourself.'

'*Cornish Princess.*'

'Stand by for boarding.'

The cutter drew alongside, and a figure jumped from it into the boat. The figure was dressed in uniform. 'Where are you going?' he asked.

'Back to Geraint's Cove, o'course,' answered the helmsman evenly, taking out his pipe and beginning to fill it again.

'And where have you been?'

'Just a trip round. What might all this be about?'

'We're going to search your boat,' said the one wearing uniform. He turned back to the cutter. 'Blake, join me on this boat.'

Another, also in uniform, joined them.

'Help yourself. Though what you expect to find, I don't know. And make sure you leave everything as you find it,' he called as the man addressed as Blake opened the door which Colin had been told led to a lavatory.

'Yeah, put the seat down after you've used it,' said the other, and laughed.

The two, between them, searched every space on the boat which could have held as much as an envelope.

'Why don't you take up the floorboards while you're at it?' asked the helmsman, puffing at his pipe steadily.

The one who had boarded them first did not answer. 'Found anything?' he demanded of Blake.

'Nothing there, Sir.'

'Very well. Thank you for your co-operation, gentlemen.' He looked queerly at Colin before they climbed back to their own craft.

'Can we go now?' asked the helmsman.

'As soon as you are showing the correct lights,' was the reply.

'Aye, aye, *Sir*,' said the helmsman heavily, switched them on, and as the two boats drew away from each other the cutter extinguished its searchlights, which faded rapidly through yellow to a red glow and then disappeared altogether. Then the engines roared a little as it moved off under the power of its twin screws. The *Cornish Princess* pulled away more sluggishly.

'What was all that about?' asked Colin.

'Aah, trying it on, to catch us out. But they'll have a hard job to catch us, I'm telling you. Don't you take no notice of 'em, lad. Anyway—' and he smiled for the first time— you've had a nice bit o' excitement on your first trip. But if I was you, you'd better not breathe a word to your great-aunt. It—er—wouldn't go so well for you, I expect, if she got to hear so much as a whisper about it.'

Then there was silence again, and another pouring of tea from the flask, and after that the two boatmen seemed to have lost interest in Colin until in the darkness far ahead he could see yellowish lights, which might have been car headlamps. The man with the pipe saw them, too, and at once slowed his engine.

'And here's where you get off,' he grunted. 'Not far now.'

The other man nipped agilely to the stern and drew the dinghy carefully round to the side. Colin looked about him, and withdrew the step-ladder and having seen how it hooked over the side fixed it firmly. Then he lowered himself cautiously into the rowing boat and sat down at once to keep it stable.

'You all right?'

'I think so.'

'Then you're on your own.' The rope was thrown into the dinghy and the rowing boat drifted a few feet while Colin sorted out the oars, and the *Cornish Princess* departed. Colin rowed towards the shore, where he could see a light waving from side to side.

TEN

THE ARTIST LEAVES HURRIEDLY

Colin spent the morning cleaning the cottage like a house-wife expecting visitors, dusting everything, vacuum-cleaning the carpets, shaking rugs, changing the bedclothes, all at great speed so as to get the job done. He knew how to make a bed, because of long practice at home to assist his mother, but he was glad that none of the village boys could see him doing it, or they would have thought he was a girl for certain.

Aunt Daphne was taking his mother out for another visit early that afternoon, on a bus to Falmouth. This time Colin had declined to go, because it was going to be more of a shopping expedition, from all accounts, although how his great-aunt was going to shop on crutches he was not sure. She had certainly made rapid progress during the last day and a half, ever since she had attempted to use a walking-stick, and he thought the reason might be that she was deter-minded to return to using that stick as soon as possible and get rid of her cumbersome crutches. She had been swinging about the house on them as if they had become part of her—but as for accompanying her with her crutches round the shops, that was out!

Aunt Daphne seemed to understand exactly his attitude, and was obviously amused by it. She gave the impression that it would have been her attitude, too, if they had somehow changed places and ages. They had an early meal, then she and his mother caught the bus which ran through the village, to change at Penzance for the one to Falmouth, while Colin performed his other duty of washing the dishes.

'We two shall have tea in Falmouth,' his mother said. 'Now don't you forget the time and go without yours.' Then she had kissed him—another thing he was glad the boys of the village did not see—and he was on his own.

Fred was out—something to do with a tractor, he was told when he went to call for him. There were no other boys around, so most likely they were engaged on other matters of a similar nature. It had struck Colin before that there were seldom many boys round the village when he went to look for them, and hardly any girls anywhere. The first was no doubt because they were helping out on the farms earning a little extra pocket money, and the second he had already realized—there just weren't many girls who lived in Geraint's Cove anyway. Fred would be back in time for the cows later on, he had been told, but he couldn't wait until then so decided to set off by himself.

First he went to the cottage to collect his things, but then he paused and stripped off his shirt before leaving again to examine himself in a mirror. No, the bruises were hardly noticeable, so it was all right, there'd be no odd looks from tourists. He put his bathers on underneath his jeans and collected a towel and walked slowly off towards the beach. After a few yards he retraced his steps and when he emerged a second time he wore no shirt, like any other village boy. He cast a few careless glances at the sky, but it was still clear and blue.

He had been sunbathing for some time when a shadow fell over him and remained there. He opened his eyes to see the artist standing before him.

'Ah, the one who found my ring for me,' he said.

Colin blinked and then realized that the man was making out that he had had no other contact with him, no doubt in case anyone was listening. Colin sat up and looked around. The man sat beside him, with his hands clasped round his knees, apparently having come to the same conclusion as Colin that there was no one on the beach whom he recognized.

'You were in the church,' said Colin in a low voice just in case. 'Didn't you see me?'

'There were a lot of others around at the time.' That seemed a good enough explanation under the circumstances, although Colin had yet to work out just what the circumstances were which made the man act like a conspirator.

'There was a bit of excitement around here last night, I hear,' continued the artist.

At Colin's raised eyebrows, the man added meaningly that he did not mean on the beach, but at sea, so Colin looked across the water innocently.

'Boats bearing down on each other, searchlights flashing in all directions, shouts and commands being given, boats being stopped and searched. Did you enjoy it?'

'I wasn't watching through the glasses last night,' said Colin.

'No, you were there,' said the artist, looking round again as if casually before he spoke.

'How do you know?' Colin asked unguardedly.

'I know most things that happen in and around this village. Just a few I don't.'

'What you mean is,' said Colin with a glimpse of understanding, 'that you were at the harbour last night, metal-detecting, when you saw the motor boat set out. Then you climbed the hill to watch.'

The artist grinned. 'Could be.' Then he spoiled the effect, and Colin could not be sure that he did not do so deliberately, by adding: 'But there was nothing they were looking for on board.'

That put a different complexion on it.

'You know a lot, for someone who's only just arrived here,' remarked Colin, and the other made no answer. 'Painted any more pictures lately?' Colin continued mischievously. 'I should think you wouldn't have had much time, what with finding lost money and snooping around.'

'Sold one,' said the man nonchalantly, 'but I haven't done any more yet.'

'How much did you get for it?'

'It was the dark, dreary scene which you saw on the easel, and I got sixty pounds.'

Colin whistled in admiration. Whatever else could be said about this fraud, he talked straight, almost like one of the village boys, even if, also like them, he had something in the background which he wanted kept hidden. What Colin had expected was to be told to mind his own business.

'Anything else you can tell me?' asked the man, as if somehow Colin had given him information instead of the other way round.

Colin shook his head. This man might have climbed the hill and seen him join the *Cornish Princess,* but by the time they had returned in the dark, nothing would have been visible out at sea from the land, he was thinking. Therefore this man must somehow be connected with the smugglers. Unless, of course, he had waited and had seen the searchlights come on and had guessed what had happened—but that would not do. Whatever he might have seen, he could not have been sure that the boat from the harbour had been stopped, because it might have been any boat out there. Perhaps it was because of the hot afternoon, but a sort of shutter clicked down in Colin's brain so that he was not able to think things out as clearly as he would have liked. There was a curtain fallen across, through which daylight could be seen but nothing with clarity.

The only thing which was emerging was that either this man was something to do with local smugglers, or he was against them. If he were connected with them, he must be someone very powerful in the background. It might even be that he was the brains or the money behind it. If he was against them, then that might explain why he was secretly watching the activities that night when Colin had stowed away in the dinghy and then had run away. He chose to risk one more attempt, for he had nothing to lose.

'I know one thing,' Colin said slowly, finding himself falling into an imitation of the slow drawl of the Cornish boys, 'and that is, you're not an artist.'

'Are you casting aspersions on my undoubted talent?' asked the man with some amusement.

'No. Stating a fact. You got those pictures in your studio from St Ives.'

The other brushed the suggestion away and reminded Colin that he had seen wet paint on the picture which had been resting against the easel.

'Yeah, the finishing touches only. I was in St Ives when I saw you in the studio near the sea front, and when you loaded them into your van. It was the same time as Mr Trewan was in St Ives, talking to a boatman by the harbour.

The supposed artist sat upright suddenly, as if he had been stung unexpectedly, and ceased to look anything but deadly serious all at once. 'Trewan was in St Ives?' He spoke very quietly, more out of the side of his mouth, when his lips were seen to move at all. He was obviously thinking deeply. 'Did you see where he went, either before or after?'

'No. I was just coming out of the lifeboat station when I noticed him. He wouldn't have seen you with the real artist, or at any rate I don't think so.'

There was another long pause for thought. Around them, there were the sounds of surf breaking gently from the near distance, and of many voices all talking at once as the visitors chatted indistinguishably to each other in family groups, and from somewhere a baby or small child was crying. Some seagulls were overhead, flying or sitting on the rocks and making a shrill din, and Colin brushed away a wasp which was manoeuvring in search of a faint smell of orange peel and buzzing near his head. Shouts of children came from the sea.

'I'll have to leave you,' said the artist, standing up. Then as he bent down to pick up a handkerchief which he had dropped he said closer to Colin's ear: 'You've hardly met me, and we've hardly spoken. Keep your mouth shut about everything—to everybody. Right?'

The handkerchief reminded Colin of something. 'How's your arm?' he asked, noticing that the man was wearing a long-sleeved shirt.

'I'll tell you about that sometime.' Then he was gone.

It must have been about four o'clock, after Colin had been into the sea again and was drying in the sun, that Mark appeared within his vision, looking rather fierce.

'You're wanted,' he said.

ELEVEN

THE TRIAL OF TERROR

When Mark led him towards the café, at first Colin thought that Derek wanted to see him about something or other round the back of the car park, perhaps, but they passed the café, with its customers queueing outside as usual and its house standing just a little way beyond it, walked up the road and then turned off into the two fields and headed in the direction of the clump of trees. He could see among the trees maybe half of the boys gathered, and among them was Derek, who was standing looking towards himself and Mark.

'Funny time for a meeting,' observed Colin amiably.

'Everybody below,' ordered Derek, and obediently the boys one after the other descended the hole into the underground passage, until finally there was only Derek, Mark and himself outside. 'And you,' said Derek grimly, and Colin found himself below with the rest.

Then Mark entered, followed by Derek who swung himself through the stone framework with a practised ease. Mark seemed to be remaining inside the lintels on guard. The rest had gathered down the passageway at the mouth of the chambers on the right and drew back a little as Colin tried to join them.

'Lights,' said Derek, and matches flared as three candles gave a yellow glow into the gloom, reflecting on the expectant faces. They were all crouching down or sitting on the ground. 'The trial will now begin,' said Derek.

Colin glanced around. Fred was not to be seen. Presumably he was looking after the cows, since it was time, or still with the tractor. Simon was not present, either. From the positions of the others, however, it was clear whose trial was being held. There was a look of anticipation on the faces surrounding him, and Colin felt uncomfortable inside himself. Derek stepped forward into the candlelight. It was hard to believe that it was bright sunlight outside, for down here it was cool, specially for one not wearing a shirt. He noticed that there were no longer any barrels standing against the wall of the chamber.

'Welcome to our secret hide-out,' leered Derek to Colin.

'What's it all about?' asked Colin. His hair was still wet from the sea water, and his head felt cold.

'You,' said Derek briefly. 'Evidence, somebody.'

A figure stepped forward into the semi-circle, bent double because of the low ceiling. It was one of those to whom Colin had paid hardly any attention before, a fairly tall, thin boy with a large, loose mouth. 'He was coming out of that artist's place down by the harbour, when it was dark, the other night. I was round there at the time and saw him come out, but he didn't see me.'

So this gangling youth had been the shadow he thought he had seen in the darkness. 'The studio was open, so I went to have a look at his pictures,' said Colin bravely. 'What's wrong with that?'

'You were also seen talking to him on the beach, some days ago,' said another voice.

Colin thought. 'Oh, yes. He'd lost a ring in the sand and I found it for him. I'd never seen him before.'

Then: 'You've also spoken to him at the harbour, on the sandy bit at low tide.'

'So what?' asked Colin stoutly. 'What's so special about him? There some law or something about speaking to people?'

'When you went to church with your dear mother and your Aunt Daphne,' said Derek. 'I noticed that you pretended that you didn't know him. Yet you did know him.'

'And this afternoon, on the beach, you've not long ago held a very long conversation with the same person, and he got up suddenly and hurried away,' said Mark.

'So? He just got up and went.'

'You haven't got the point yet, have you? All of this makes us very suspicious,' said Derek, dragging out his words very slowly indeed. 'You talk to this stranger, and you talk to him a lot, and then you pretend that you don't know him afterwards, and he pretends that he doesn't know you. And then you know how Mark fell into the sea, and mention it in a sneaky sort of way, which you could not have known unless you or your friend had been spying.'

'That's right,' said Mark.

'And then when you go for a little row on our behalf, lo and behold there's a raid on the boat, as if somebody had been told beforehand that a little trip had been planned. There's only one stranger apart from you moved into this village for months. Now what have you got to say?'

The only matters which these did not seem to know was that he already knew of the existence of these underground chambers, and that he had found a barrel hidden at the farm. Certainly, then, Fred had not talked. Also they did not know that he had spent a night at the studio. Had they known that, his guilt would have been proved beyond all doubt.

'Well, I've told him nothing,' lied Colin. 'I don't know this man at all. Never met him before. But he seems pleasant enough. Added to which, I don't know anything to tell him even if I wanted to, do I?'

He seemed to have scored a point there, but it was only a temporary triumph. Derek announced that there was something fishy, nevertheless, and if only by implication invited Colin to say more. Colin said quietly that if they intended to beat him up again on such trumped-up evidence he'd go straight to the police.

There was an indrawing of breath from all around him, and an excited chatter broke out. Colin had made a mistake in saying that, he was sure now. Derek nodded and everybody left the passage except for himself and Colin, as at a pre-arranged signal. Mark, he noticed, was still squatting at the narrow entrance, but apart from the three of them within a minute the place was deserted. The candles still flickered.

'You have to be taught a lesson,' hissed Derek. 'You'd better sit on the floor for a minute.' He kneeled down in front of him and from somewhere round his back fumbled and produced a large, wooden-handled sheath knife which he held in front of him menacingly. The blade was perhaps six inches long, gleamed in the light and was definitely very sharp.

'Going to the police would not be a good idea at all. We couldn't afford for you to do that. Do you know what we do to people who tell tales when they shouldn't?' He drew his face closer to Colin's until they were only a few inches apart and Colin could smell his smoky breath. 'You know what happened to Simon? We made him break his arm. And that was only for saying very little.'

'You mean you intended to break his arm?' Colin was aghast.

'Either that or hit his head on the rock in the pool and kill himself,' breathed Derek. 'But perhaps you have heard, if you remember, about somebody else who once talked. Did anyone tell you what really happened to him?'

'He—he fell off a cliff,' said Colin, 'I think.'

'Ye-e-s, fell off a cliff. And where is he now?'

Colin shrugged helplessly. From the distance he could hear a little snigger from Mark.

'Not with us any more. Not in this world at all. There's a little spot in the churchyard where what's left of him is properly laid. But one part is still missing. It got cut off. Nobody knew how it had happened when his body got washed up on the rocks later. Do you know what was missing?'

Colin shook his head and tried to draw his face further away from the other, but Derek put one hand behind his head and pulled him nearer.

'When the body was recovered, one hand wasn't there any more. It was almost as if it had been cut off with a knife—like this one.' He waved the blade slowly from side to side before Colin's terrified eyes. 'Very tragic, it was. Something hungry in the sea must have eaten it, eh? Except for one thing. We all know that he lost his hand *before* he fell off the cliff, not afterwards. You see, we knew that he had been talking, so we dragged him down here, something like you've been brought down here, except you came of your own free will, as if you were coming for a treat. And when he was safely down here, and he couldn't escape, we put a gag in his mouth so he couldn't shout out. His own hankie, it was,' he said contemplatively as if savouring the memory of the scene. 'And then—with a knife, perhaps this one here, he accidentally had his left hand sawn off. He couldn't scream, you see, not with a mouth full of cloth.'

Then Derek laughed, not a laugh of humour but a weird sound of inward pleasure, an unpleasant noise which seemed to gurgle and hiss in his throat.

'It took us a long time to get it right off. We buried it somewhere at this end of the hideout—over there by that wall, I think, yes, right by the wall—while he watched us do it.'

Involuntarily Colin's eyes swivelled towards the fearful spot. Derek was mad. He was mad and evil, there was now no doubt at all. From the manner in which Derek was telling him, he was gloating over the details of the horrific account, as if even the retelling gave him intense pleasure. Colin turned his eyes back towards the face in front of him.

'Then we kept the gag in his mouth, and he was moaning and dripping blood all the way to the cliff. And that was when we threw him over.'

He moved the knife blade closer to Colin's face, and Colin tried to draw away, only to find that Derek's hand was still firmly at the back of his head.

'No, we're not going to do anything to you just yet. I'm

114

going to leave you for some time to think how foolish it would be if you said anything ever again, or how dangerous it could be for you if you even thought of telling the police. After all—'

And Colin knew that what he had left unsaid was that if he had to be arrested for one death, it would make no difference if he were found guilty of two. Colin shuddered.

'I won't talk,' he said, much more loudly than he had intended.

Derek laughed the same sinister sound again. 'I'll give you a chance to think about it. You can stay for quite a while. Your mother and Mrs Johnson are out till late, aren't they, so you won't be missed for a long time yet? And who knows? —I might even let you go before they return, if I think it's worth it. If you dig around carefully, you might even find the hand we cut off your predecessor. Then when we come back, I'll decide what to do with you. I might—only might, mind —let you go so you can think of what will happen to you at any time I choose.'

Then he blew out the candles and crept towards the entrance, his knife still grasped in his right hand. Mark left the passage, followed by Derek, and Colin heard sounds coming from outside. There was a sudden rumble, and the passage was in total darkness. The boys had rolled a rock of some sort over the entrance. There was silence.

When Derek had gone, Colin remained sitting on the ground, quite still, for several minutes. His legs were trembling a little, and his hands. Then he lifted one arm and touched the roof above him, and raised himself up and felt his way towards the entrance hole, which he found securely blocked. Try as he might he could not push away the rough stone nor pull pieces through the hole towards him. There was just a slight gap, but so slight that it barely let light through. At least this meant that if he was careful he would not suffocate. The stone then did move a fraction, and he guessed that after the first rock had been dropped the boys had barricaded it from the other side with more, so if he rocked it a little. . . .

Rocking, however, was useless, for the stones pressing against it had nowhere else to fall, and only served to wedge it more firmly. He was alone in the blackness in a low, dark tunnel, with no possible way of escape. Nobody ever talked about this passage, Aunt Daphne had said, so that tourists would not swarm all over it. That meant that nobody ever came here, then, apart from the boys—and whoever had put the barrels down and taken them out again. He could be here for days, and no one would think of searching. He was, to all intents, buried alive!

The atmosphere in the place was oppressive, for it was low as well as dark, and only if he lay full-length on the floor would he be able to stretch his limbs. A claustrophobic attack come over him, the fear of being in a confined space, and for a few seconds he found it difficult to breathe until he reasoned with himself that the air could not be running out, and would not for a very long time, if at all. Then he recovered his senses, sat down by the only escape, which was now of no use to him whatever, and tried to think things out. He shut his eyes.

The passage was not likely to cave in on him, that was the first thing. It had stood for centuries, and was not going to collapse now. He had enough air. He could not get out, not until he had thought of some way of loosening the stone in the blocked doorway anyway, and that might take a long time. He could be left there until he starved to death, if Derek chose. But that would take several days, he would expect. There could be another consignment of barrels before that happened. He would not freeze, he thought, even if there was a cold night, for in any case it was not freezing weather, and even if there was a cold night he would think that the temperature down there remained pretty constant, being underground. It was fairly cool now, but he did not anticipate that it would grow very much colder.

As he considered his unpleasant situation, he came to a

calm conclusion. Either Derek had been lying, and the boy who had fallen over the cliff had not had his hand cut off first, in which case he had merely been trying to frighten him—or Derek had not been lying, and he really had killed the boy, had cut off his hand with his knife, and when eventually he returned to the passage might have a go at killing him as well. Certainly Derek had seemed inhuman not many minutes before, as if there was some demon of violence inside him which was struggling to get out. Derek could be dangerous, he was sure. On the other hand, he might have been acting.

Now he felt much calmer. He opened his eyes, although they were of no use to him at all for the present, and felt his way along the wall to the chamber where the boys had been gathered. There was still a smell of candle wax lingering in the air.

He had nothing else to do for the moment, so he would test which of the theories, whether Derek was a killer or whether he was not, was the true one. First, though, he wanted to find his towel with his bathers wrapped in it. He felt around on the ground until he found his trunks, still wet through, but the towel must be elsewhere. The two items had become separated in the disturbance, he supposed. Keeping his swimming gear in his hand, he felt around with the other, until he made contact with the towel right against the wall of the chamber, and wrapped the one inside the other, laying the damp bundle carefully where he knew he could find it again.

Then he stretched out his arms to locate his position, and when he was sure where he was, kneeled down and started scratching at the soil at the base of the chamber wall, beginning on the left just where it began to curve. If Derek had been telling the truth, which on the face of it was unlikely, he would find a buried hand hidden in the soil. And if he couldn't find the gruesome relic, Derek had been trying to frighten him. It was as simple as that. And now that he could reason things out a little more rationally, he would like to bet that he would find nothing, no matter for how long he searched. He had plenty of time, so he would make a good job of it.

Only having fingers to do the job, he took care not to hurt himself. Nobody ever actually walked right against the stone which marked the end of the passage system, so if anything had been buried the ground would not have been pressed hard afterwards. The barrels might have compressed the soil, admittedly, and what he was digging into now was very firm and difficult to scrabble out. So that meant no hole had been dug out there, he supposed.

He worked his way round the curve of the chamber slowly and carefully. Where he found the soil extra-hard, he assumed that it had been hard for centuries, and leaving that part moved on a little. It was just as he had expected, the ground was almost rock-hard everywhere. Nobody had been digging there, that was for certain. The boys—or murderers—would not have taken a spade underground with them, so any hole would have been piggled out with a knife, or at any rate nothing larger than a trowel, and also the hole would not have been very deep.

As he searched, the more he became convinced that Derek had been trying to panic him. There was nothing except—

Then he came to a little section of soil which felt soft to the touch of his finger-tips. It was about four inches wide and perhaps six or seven inches long. He stopped, and took a deep breath. Then he touched it tentatively a second time. There was no mistake, it was soft soil underneath his hand, just short of half-way round the end of the chamber as far as he could judge. His eyes opened wide, trying to strain for any light in the darkness, but there was none. He began to dig furiously, in a panic of activity, his heart beginning to thump a little, scooping out the soil not into a mound but in any direction as long as he could continue to dig down with his bare hands. He heard rather than felt fragments of soil land on the legs of his jeans, brushed them off and dug again, with both hands, one after the other.

He felt something with the tip of one finger. Whatever it was felt narrow and hard, and was a few inches long. He dug round it and below it, then plunged his hand in and grasped what he could of the object. It came out in his hand, and he felt it cautiously, reluctantly with the other one.

With a cry of despair he flung the thing away from him into the darkness and sat back on his haunches petrified with horror. He had touched the decayed skeleton of a human hand!

TWELVE

THE FULLY-FLEDGED CONSPIRATOR

He sat huddled in a corner of the chamber at the end of the passage, and he found himself crying with fright. Little children cry for a variety of reasons—from shock, with temper, from cold, with despair, to obtain their own way or simply to attract attention. Older children cry because of grief, because of pain, or because of humiliation or despair. Those who are still older might cry through grief, or because they feel sorry for themselves. Rarely do they cry from fright. Terror petrifies, makes those who have come to a situation where a false step might result in death grip tightly and not dare to move, makes those in great danger freeze in horror at an impending doom, like rabbits—or it makes them run away.

Down in the underground passage, however, Colin was free to move safely. There was no risk of falling from a great height, no sudden enemy, no wild animal about to attack, no advancing machine to run him over and crush him. There was nothing from which he could run and escape, for there was nothing tangible. He was in no immediate danger, and nowhere could he run. Therefore the cold thought of what had happened to that other boy, whoever he had been, made him huddle against the wall. He wondered how old he had been, and whether he had had any brothers or sisters, or whether he had a widowed mother, as Colin had, and whether she had remained in the village with its memories or had left to leave the memories behind. The tears were for his mother, who would be left alone, and for himself, because he was feeling sorry for himself.

It would not do. He certainly could not give up so easily. If Derek came at him with his knife, he would have to make sure that he did not win an easy victory but would receive marks on him which would need explanation. Added to which, Derek couldn't kill him down there and leave him. His body would have to be carried somewhere else, because the ground would be too hard to dig up and bury him in it, and that would need to be done secretly, in the dark, and with assistance from others.

He stopped crying and thought. His great-aunt had said that perhaps this passage at some time had been used for people hiding from their enemies. Now this was likely, because the narrow entrance would enable anyone inside to fight fiercely against those who discovered it and tried to come in. Only one at a time could try to get in. One person inside ought to be able to hold off anyone from outside. It would be like Horatius on the bridge, where in Roman times he and two friends held off the entire enemy army because the bridge over the River Tiber was so narrow. It was like Leonidas at the Pass of Thermopylae, when the King of Sparta and a small group of soldiers held off an enormous army because the pass was so narrow that they could do this.

With more determination now, he felt his way along the wall to the blocked entrance and considered his plan. If Derek came with the intention of hurting him, he would expect to find him drawing back or even scuttling off to the far end of the passage. Then Derek would follow him, corner him, and then either by himself or in the company of some of the other boys—he bet they would be Mark and that gangling boy with the slack mouth—he would be able to do just as he liked.

But if Colin stayed near the entrance, and instead of retreating attacked each one as they tried to step down through the hole, he might get hurt a bit, even receive the odd slight cut, but nobody would be able to get in. Now to enter one had to come in feet first. If he grabbed hold of the legs of anyone who attempted to enter, and pulled, the intruder would be flat on his back and helpless, and before he would have time to recover he would be the attacker and the other would be at his mercy. And with one in trouble, the others would think twice before they tried to follow.

He would frighten them out of their wits for a start, if they saw that he intended to fight and was not fussy about the methods he used. That was how to tackle the problem, there was no doubt. He would start preparing now. It would just be a matter of timing, and moving fast when the time came.

Now the effort of thought put him completely over his misery and his fright, and both emotions were replaced by a single, cold logic. He wondered if they had ever seen the skeleton of a human hand before. He doubted it. He would fling that in their faces for a start. Without giving his courage time to falter, he hurried back as fast as the dark would allow to the chamber at the end of the tunnel and searched around for the hand, and when he found it, realized that by itself it was not an object of revulsion. He ran his fingers over it, not able to see it but discovering its outline by careful touch. For a boy's, it was quite a large hand, and the bones were smooth. There was a nail at the end of each finger, firmly attached and a little long, and he fell to considering what sort of boy this had been—pretty tall, careful not to soil his finger nails, and most likely of a slender build because the hand was narrow. Then he recovered his damp towel also and moved himself and the two articles to the wall opposite the entrance to await future events.

It must have been well over two hours later when he heard a scrambling of feet outside, and soft chink of rocks being removed. A fragment of dim light began to appear, which enlarged as more of the material blocking the entrance was taken away. Finally he heard a voice say, 'Come on—lift,' and the stone fell back, and then was raised out of the hole outside. He saw a pair of legs wearing jeans scramble out of the hole, to be replaced with a different pair of legs. The time had at last come!

'Had enough?' enquired a silky voice which was Derek's.

'Come in and get me,' said Colin, crouching, ready to spring, against the opposite wall, 'but first have this.'

He flung the skeletal hand out through the opening and was very satisfied to see it land on the face of the boy outside.

'Glad you bothered to find it,' said Derek. There was a snigger from somewhere above and behind him, and Colin recognized the sound as belonging to Mark. There did not seem to be anyone with them. 'Now have it back!' And the bones of the hand come straight back at Colin. 'And now you can see, have a good look at it.'

The repulsive object now lay on the ground at the side of Colin.

'Go on—pick it up and have a good look at it.'

Keeping a wary eyes on the opening, Colin reached down and raised the bones nearer to his face. They were a grey-green colour. He shook them, and the fingers wobbled at the end of the bones of the hand. He held the hand in both of his and inspected it wonderingly. It was the sort which could be purchased in any joke shop, and was made of plastic.

Derek burst out laughing. 'Do you really think I'd cut a kid's hand off?' he demanded among bursts of hilarity. 'Come on up, Ginger, you've had your lesson.'

Crestfallen, Colin began to scramble out, and Mark put out a hand to help him, which Colin accepted. They sat on the bank at the top of the hole, with their legs dangling into it.

'If you'd have been snivelling at the end of the passage, I'd have frightened you some more,' said Derek unpleasantly, 'but you showed spirit all right. I thought you'd set about seeing if what I had said was the truth, and then come to the conclusion that it was. So you've had your punishment.'

He laughed again, and Colin joined in a little shame-facedly, but not for long. There was still something distinctly rotten about Derek, and about Mark for that matter. Whether this was a joke or not, it had been anything but funny at the time, as Derek well knew. Added to that, there was still the time when he had been beaten up, and he was not going to forget, or forgive, that in a hurry.

'Now be reasonable,' said Derek. 'Stop trying to find out what doesn't concern you. Stop telling anyone else, even by hinting, what little you know. More things go on around here than you could dream of in your tiny city mind, and nobody wants it spoiled. If certain matters leaked out, some people you see, wouldn't find it very amusing, and a lot could get into trouble if snoopers came.

'You're not here in the village for very long. So just join in and enjoy it, and when you get home again, just forget all about it. Then if you come again another year, you can belong like the rest of us again.'

Then he said a very curious thing : 'But what I said earlier still goes. You don't talk when you get back to Birmingham. We really do have friends there, and it really wouldn't be healthy. *They* won't play games.'

'You don't play games round here, either,' said Colin while rapid thoughts were ticking over in his mind. The artist and his wound came uppermost to mind with considerable clarity as they coincided with a memory of what had sounded like the back-firing of a car. He thought he understood a little more now, and did not like what he understood.

'We don't play games with strangers,' said Derek. 'They ask for all they get. But you aren't really a stranger.'

Mark had said not a word. He was sitting like an age-old stone on the edge of the pit, but Colin could hear him breathing. Now he spoke : 'Next time, we shan't play games with you, either, and don't you forget it.'

'You'd better go now,' said Derek. 'Stop thinking so much.'

Then Colin rose to his feet and began to walk across the field towards the village. 'Hey, one thing I didn't tell you, and perhaps you'd better know.'

Colin turned.

'That kid really did fall off a cliff, you know. He didn't die, but he fell all right.'

Colin ran the rest of the way. Derek was evil. It had not all been pretence. Now he was certain. He was twisted in his mind, and one day he was going to be really dangerous, the sort you read about in the papers. From behind he heard jeering laughter.

When he reached the road, he did not stop running, but looked back to find the light was just dim enough now for him to be unable to discern more than a vague outline of the clump of trees. That meant that from the trees it would be impossible to tell where he was or what he was doing. He turned down the road which led towards the harbour, and when the pace was beginning to tell on him slowed to a steady jog-trot, and while padding along felt in his back pocket to ensure that he still possessed a certain key.

By the time he arrived at the group of buildings near the harbour he was gasping for breath. He took the precaution of looking all around first, found there was nobody at all whom he recognized as a local inhabitant, then fitted the emergency key into the lock of the studio door, slipped inside and pushed the door firmly shut behind him. Then he bent forward with his hands on his knees until his heart returned to normal and his breath was easier, and only then replaced the key in his pocket.

The studio was in darkness. He stumbled across the floor to the stairs at the other end, and ran up them, and when he reached the head of the stairs flung open the door of the living quarters. He blinked at what he saw as he turned towards a movement over by the left of the door.

'I thought it would be you,' said the man, since I heard the key in the lock, but I don't take avoidable risks.'

He walked over to a jacket and put the gun back in one of the pockets.

'So now you know a lot more than you did before,' remarked the man calmly.

'How do you know I won't tell somebody?' said Colin, still standing by the door.

'You're an unavoidable risk,' was the reply. 'You did something foolhardy before you were caught by me on the beach, and if I hadn't found you, you would have been in much more trouble. I wasn't being altruistic, you know. I could have been caught if they had known about your unwelcome presence. So now you're in trouble again. Tell me.'

'Did you get shot?' demanded Colin bluntly. 'In the arm?' He was not sure what altruistic meant, but he gathered that it had some connection with not doing something just for his good.

The man seated himself on the armchair, then changed his mind and got up to close and bolt the door before re-occupying the chair. He indicated the bed, and Colin sat on the edge of it.

'Um—I received a slight graze, nothing of any importance.'

So games were not being played. It was clear now that this man, whoever he was, was on the opposite side from the smugglers, and if life was at risk the only reason could be that a huge sum of money was involved. Nobody living round there seemed especially wealthy, but there must be somebody who was collecting a great profit.

'Now—what brings you here in such a rush?'

'I've been talking to you, and what with one thing and another, everybody's putting two and two together. They suspect you, but no one's told me why.'

'So what did they do?' the man asked sharply.

Colin told him. He poured out about the barrel in the farmyard, the barrels in the underground passage, the village gang and the meetings on the beach. Then he told him about what had taken place that afternoon after the man had left the beach. The man fingered his chin periodically, nodded as he savoured each detail of the information which Colin was giving him, and when Colin had finally finished sat in smiling silence.

The boy on the bed looked at the man's face with some trepidation. The smile was unnerving. He had expected a quite different response, a shrewd, business-like glance or a sudden leap into action or a calm deliberation before formulating some clever plan. But all the man did was sit and smile at him, and apart from that did not move. It would seem that a disastrous mistake had been made. Somehow, this man belonged to the other side and now he had revealed to him every single suspicion and detail. This man could overpower him, and later at night take him out to sea and dump him into it and that would be the end of him. After all the difficulties of the previous few hours Colin could not fight any more. He had made a fool of himself, and now he had not even the will to give more than a token resistance. The man continued to smile and Colin let his body sag in hopelessness as the thoughts shot home.

Then the man stopped smiling as he saw the change in expression on Colin's face, went over and sat by him on the bed.

'You must be done in,' he said. 'Here, cheer up. I'll make us both a cup of coffee. It's not as bad as all that.'

Colin raised his face in astonishment.

'What's up? Couldn't quite work out which side I was on?' the artist asked.

Colin nodded, and brightened a little. He felt out of his depth, but it seemed after all he was all right. He was at once relieved, and his face showed it.

'That's better. Don't let anyone get you down. Now I'll see about that coffee, sweet and strong. That'll soon liven you up.'

While he busied himself with the kettle and the crockery, the man talked, and sometimes he talked soothingly and sometimes he dropped out little instructions for Colin to follow in due course, and while he talked Colin began to relax a little more.

'What you found in the two fields was a fogou,' said the man, just as the kettle boiled. 'It's a prehistoric underground passage, peculiar to Cornwall. There are about twenty of them known, that's all, each one at least as old as Stonehenge. If you ever go to Chysauster, which is on the other side of Penzance from here, there's a whole prehistoric village, with houses in rows, and all that, and what's left of a fogou on the edge of the village. But from what you've described, you've found a complete one. Now that's very unusual. You've made a valuable discovery.'

Colin brightened as he sipped the scalding coffee.

'If it got known in London, or at any of the universities, you'd have the place swarming with archaeologists before you could blink. They'd be very excited.'

Colin said that the people in the village of Geraint's Cove did not want its existence to be known to outsiders. His great-aunt had said so.

'I'm not surprised. Sounds as if they've been using it as a hiding place for contraband for centuries,' said the man, smiling again, but this time the smile seemed considerably more friendly, although in fact there was probably not the slightest difference between now and the previous occasion.

Colin said hastily that was not the reason. The man said that perhaps it wasn't the only reason, then added something to the effect that the boy was beginning to sound like a local inhabitant himself. Colin wanted to know what was wrong with smuggling anyway, and the answer was that it was robbing the Government of money.

'Oh, I know,' said the man, 'many people try to smuggle the odd item into the country without paying duty when they return from foreign holidays. You often hear those who boast of how they brought in the odd thing without paying duty on it, and that sort of affair. The Customs officers pounce on them when they catch them, but the occasional watch or bottle of perfume doesn't mean very much. But you imagine someone bringing in thousands of pounds' worth of goods—or smuggling in drugs, that sort of thing. Now you might see why smuggling has to be stopped. When you're talking about thousands of pounds, or stuff that can kill or maim—'

He broke off, and stepped swiftly over to the door and listened intently, and at once Colin's fears returned.

'No, it was nothing. Anyway, what we are going to do now is this. I shall get you home in the the back of the van. You'll be in the back so that nobody will be able to see you if we happen to pass either your friends or your enemies. When we reach a safe spot, you can get out. And then hurry off home, or you'll catch cold with no shirt on. I'll then drive on. That way, nobody will know that you've even seen me tonight.

'Now you might hear over the next day or so when the next trip is planned. It would help if you could let me know somehow. Be careful. All you need do when you happen to pass me—and I'll be around—is name a day. That's all. We know about what time, after all, don't we? Do you think that would be possible?'

Colin felt that he could manage it somehow.

'Now be careful. We're not playing games—as you know.' The smile was gone. Colin nodded again. Feeling like a conspirator well out of his apprenticeship, he eventually found himself huddled down in the back of the little green van as the man drove quickly up the hill towards the village.

THIRTEEN

FRED EXPLAINS

'You were late in last night,' said his mother, as they were leaving the cottage to walk along the road to Aunt Daphne's for breakfast. She closed the door behind them and they set off. It was a clear, bright morning with just a hint of a chill in the air. 'Where had you been?'

'Oh—just out.' He shrugged.

'All that I'm thinking of is that we aren't seeing much of you this holiday, and I'd like to know what you're getting up to.'

He flushed just slightly and wished that he had not, because he knew that mothers are not easily deceived. It was not that he wanted to be secretive, but as matters stood it would be best that his mother, and his great-aunt, did not know all of the ins, outs and complications which were arising. Fortunately, his blushing was taken to mean something else.

'It's not that I don't want you to enjoy yourself, and I know that you've made a lot of holiday friends here, but I want to make sure that you're not getting into mischief. Don't think that you're neglecting me, because I'm very happy as things are, and there's no reason for you to hang around with two women all day long. You're growing up, and it's right that you should start to lead a life of your own every now and then.'

Then she was silent, letting what she had said sink in. Within a few minutes, they were at Aunt Daphne's house and opening the door. 'But out of curiosity, I'd like to know what you did yesterday.'

'I didn't do anything,' Colin flared up without exactly intending to.

'Oh, what's this?' asked Aunt Daphne, who was not sitting down but was laying the table for breakfast. Her improvement was remarkable for her age—or her determination. 'Temper, Colin?' She gave him a schoolmistress look as if he had forgotten his homework, and he felt a faint redness appearing again.

'He was late last night,' said his mother in explanation, 'and I wanted to know where he'd been.'

'Well. . . .' he began cautiously. It would not do at all for him to speak the complete truth. 'I was down at the cove and then I saw Derek and most of the others, and we sort of hung around together until late.'

His great-aunt expressed surprise that Derek was able to take part of an afternoon off from the café without his father making a fuss. 'The Trewans are great ones for trying to make money,' she added, 'with as little effort and expense as possible. It's not like Trewan to let his son off work. Cheap labour, I should think. Not that Derek Trewan's worth paying much.'

'And then what?' demanded his mother as she set about assisting her aunt.

'Then I went down to the harbour and saw that artist who's got a studio down there, and he gave me a cup of coffee.'

'Why should he give you a cup of coffee?'

Colin shrugged for a third time. 'We were just talking.'

'But you don't know anything about him.' His mother was not, however, unduly surprised, for her son had a knack of involving himself in conversation with almost anybody.

'I found a ring for him once, which he'd lost on the beach. He goes metal-detecting down at the harbour most nights, finding money which people have lost.'

'I think that would be Mr Mitchell,' said Aunt Daphne astonishingly. 'I thought I saw him at church last Sunday, but he didn't know me. His grandfather came from these parts, then his father went off and married a girl from Truro, and that's where they lived. I heard rumours that he was back. Nobody round here would know him, of course. His father's been gone for too long.'

'Then how did you recognize him?' asked Colin.

'Got his father's look about him,' said the old lady briskly. 'I didn't know he was an artist, though, until he came back to Geraint's Cove. Ah, there's no telling nowadays.'

The talk seemed to have taken quite a different turning, and Colin was grateful that Aunt Daphne wandered down various by-lanes of memory during breakfast and the questioning had been forgotten. Then Colin washed up. Aunt Daphne had become much more sprightly this morning. The crutches were left pointedly leaning against a corner of the room while she steadied her way round the house with the aid of the furniture and her thick stick. From the kitchen, he just managed to overhear her telling his mother that she needn't worry about Colin because there was not much harm he could come to in that neighbourhood. He thought grimly that despite her amazing knowledge she didn't know everything—which was probably just as well.

He came across Fred later on in the morning, mooching around outside the house and doing nothing in particular, as if he had been hoping to see him. The two wandered off together towards the shop to buy ice cream.

'I heard about yesterday,' said Fred gloomily.

'They kept me down in the fogou,' said Colin.

'They would.' He did not seem to find anything unusual in Colin's knowing the name given to such an underground passage.

'I'd been down it before. I told you, I found it once, by accident.'

'Did you find anything hidden in it, the first time?'

'Yes.'

They entered the shop, and Colin treated Fred. They walked across to the grass near the signpost and sat down to eat.

'Well,' said Fred, 'I hope you keep your mouth shut.'

'What do you take me for? Your uncle had a barrel underneath a pile of hay or something, as well. I saw it.'

Fred grunted. 'Now you see, then, don't you? If anyone talks, everybody's in trouble.'

'But what does everyone do it for?'

Fred looked at him and explained, very slowly and cautiously. Cornwall was not a wealthy county, and most of it never had been. At one time, some Cornishmen used to lure passing cargo ships on to the rocks by putting up false lights to be mistaken for harbour lights, then when the ships were wrecked, they used to rob them. That was bad. But he remembered an old vicar explaining to him that while most people would not do that, if any ship were wrecked by accident, everybody in a village would go down to the rocks and take what they could. They had to, or starve, for there was nothing else for them. The farming was not very good, because the ground was too rocky. Not much topsoil, you see, because of the rocks being so near the surface. There was one farmer just outside the village, whom Fred could remember, always used to walk his cows down the road very slowly, so they could eat off the hedges as they passed, so he would not have to spend so much on feed for them. So a little bit of smuggling made extra cash. Besides, many Cornish people always thought of themselves as Celts, like the Scots and the Welsh, and not English at all, so it didn't seem so bad. It had got out of hand now, though. Derek had organized them. It had been fun at first, but now it had got too big.

Colin thought to himself that Derek had not the brains to organize the whole thing, and wondered who organized Derek. Perhaps it was the two men who owned the *Cornish Princess*.

'So nearly all of us are in it up to our necks,' concluded Fred. 'And if one gets caught, we all get caught.'

'Who says so?'

Fred glanced around carefully, as he had done once or twice while he had been talking, to make sure they were not being overheard.

'Derek says so. And we think he's right.'

They had finished the ice cream. Fred had ceased opening his heart, and Colin stood up.

'There's one other thing,' said Fred hesitantly, joining him. 'Don't go down to the cove tonight. Or the harbour, either. Stay in and watch the telly.'

'Something big?'

'Don't ask questions. But I've been told that tonight is the last of the season. So it'd be best if you weren't there. There'll be a meeting at the pool, but you find some reason not to go.'

Colin thought that would make Derek and Mark suspicious. Fred said that nobody could prove anything, as long as Colin stayed in and didn't go anywhere else. Then they saw Simon in the distance wearing a clean white sling, so they joined him as if they had wanted to, and presently wandered off to the harbour area, which as usual at that time of day was crowded with holidaymakers even though the *Six Lobsters* was closed. Even Mr Mitchell was busy—at least, he was handing to a woman who was loudly an American tourist a large rectangular brown-paper parcel, and she was in return giving him a small bundle of bank notes. Several other people were inspecting his stock inside the studio, and Colin observed a gap where one of the better paintings had been.

Fred and Simon were ambling along aimlessly towards the water, leaving Colin alone for a moment.

'Good morning,' said Mr Mitchell cheerily as he noticed him. 'Want to buy a picture?'

'No, thanks, I can't afford one until *tonight*,' said Colin heavily.

'Why, coming into money then?' Obviously he had not

gathered what Colin was saying. The boy tried again.

'It's just that *tonight* would be the time.'

There was a pause, as Colin moved very slowly away. The American lady, who had been listening in obvious perplexity, commented that it had been a very odd thing for the boy to say. Did it mean something different to these quaint Cornish people? The man suddenly seemed to have realized himself what a queer statement had been made, but Colin had not been able to think up anything better on the spur of the moment.

'The children round here do speak a little oddly,' he said vaguely, then Fred and Simon had turned round and were coming back for Colin, so Colin hurried on after them, burbling that the artist had just sold a picture for more than fifty pounds and expressing astonishment that he should have received so much.

When the three of them passed by the studio door again, about an hour later, it was closed and the door was shut firmly. Colin hoped that this meant that his message had been received and understood.

In the afternoon, he went into Penzance with his mother and his great-aunt. There was no bus out, so Aunt Daphne had ordered a car to take them and they would catch the bus back. Now they were having tea in a restaurant overlooking the promenade and Mounts Bay, and the light was bright and clear, and Colin suddenly had the thought of how he would regret having to return to Birmingham with its noise and traffic fumes and crowds, and how much he would have preferred to stay in the south-west permanently. But if somehow they could ever manage this, when he left school in a few years' time what would he do for a job? What he could recall most clearly of Birmingham at the moment were his own home, and the statues of Watt, Boulton and Murdoch standing outside the Register Office with a large scroll in their hands as if it were a map and they had lost their way round the city. He wasn't surprised.

His mother and Aunt Daphne were chatting and his attention wandered. Aunt Daphne did not seem to be particularly poor, despite what Fred had told him about the people in the village. It was true that her home was small, but it was expensively furnished. Even her holiday cottage, which normally she would have let out to others, was fitted with new furniture. And he knew that she had paid the rail fares of both himself and his mother to go and stay with her. And she would hire a car when she felt like it. He and his mother would not dream even of hiring a taxi unless it was a dire emergency, and they had never encountered one dire enough yet. Perhaps his great-aunt's husband had been well-to-do? Or was the old lady one of those involved in making money out of smuggling, or even the one behind it all?

He pulled himself up short. That was quite out of the question. He found Aunt Daphne pressing him to have another cake and saying that he ought to enjoy himself for once since it meant he would not have to do the washing-up. He looked into her shrewd, twinkling eyes and realized that she would certainly not be involved in activities where interlopers were shot at or where boys fell off a cliff because they talked out of turn. He decided to stay in when they returned and watch the television, as he had been advised.

FOURTEEN

THE BIG NIGHT

He was watching the television when the knock came at the door. It was eight o'clock. For safety he was at his great-aunt's cottage, so that if need be he would have witnesses that he had not gone elsewhere. His mother answered the door.

'Colin,' she called, 'it's someone for you.' Then she returned to her viewing, for the programme had just started.

'Are you coming out?' asked Mark bluntly. Behind him could be seen quite a crowd of the others, carrying towels.

Colin shook his head.

'Who is it?' called Aunt Daphne.

'Just some friends,' Colin turned his head and called back in the house.

There was a shuffling and then behind him, to the obvious surprise of the boys at the door, appeared the figure of Aunt Daphne, leaning heavily on her stick.

'Hello, Mrs Johnson,' said Mark. 'We were just wondering if Colin would like to come out and play.'

'Hello, Mark,' said the old lady. 'When you get home, tell your mother I've found that recipe for beetroot chutney which she wanted. Yes, of course he can come out, much better for him than staying in the house watching television on a nice evening.'

'Is your leg getting better, Mrs Johnson?' asked Mark ever so politely.

'Much better, thank you. Well, go on, Colin, and enjoy

yourself while you can.' She stomped back inside the house, and her great-nephew had no real choice.

The boys did not seem to be unfriendly. Fred was among them, and at a surreptitious glance which he caught and understood he raised his shoulders slightly in a gesture which indicated that he had not been able to prevent it. Clearly everyone was going to the pool, and Colin was required to accompany them with his bathers and his towel in the usual way, despite Fred's earlier warning. After the group had left the house, Mark did not speak to him again.

Derek was waiting by the pool when they arrived. This time he did not perform the diving ritual—he was fully-dressed and was sitting on the rocks. They gathered round, and he stood up and leaning against a rock lit a cigarette.

'Right, you lot, we're going to be busy tonight. You're here to get wet, so everyone will think that we've been playing about as usual. So when you're ready, strip off and get into the water. In half an hour to an hour, get out and dry yourselves, so when you get home again mummies and daddies will know that we've all been swimming as normal. Most of you know that this is the big night, and there's a lot to do, so we're starting early. Ginger, get into the water and then come out again, because you're wanted now.'

The cove was deserted apart from the excited boys. Wondering why he should be singled out, Colin entered the pool, swam around for a minute and then emerged. Derek remained by the rock, then when his cigarette was finished he threw it away.

'Okay, dry yourself, get dressed and come over to the cave. There's work for you tonight.'

'Waste of time going in, then.'

'You'd got to wet yourself by going in, so your bathers and towel will look right when you get home. We don't want your dear mother and Mrs Johnson suspicious, now, do we? We've tried dipping things in the water before, and they don't come out right.'

138

Well, that proved one thing—Aunt Daphne did not have anything to do with the smuggling.

'I'll give you five minutes, that's all.' Derek had set off to the cave.

When Colin arrived, Derek had already taken the tarpaulin off the dinghy and he could see that the outboard motor had been fitted to the bracket on the stern, tilted up just now so that it would not drag on the sand when the boat was hauled. He helped Derek pull it into the sea, then when they were both of them on board Derek sat in the stern, lowered the outboard and started the engine by pulling on the winding cord. At the second jerk the engine fired, and they were heading out to sea.

'Why me?' asked Colin in mystification.

'Insurance,' Derek said laconically, lighting yet another cigarette. 'Tonight's the big night, and as you're taking part in it, it means that you're involved right up to your neck. That'll keep your mouth shut, won't it? You wouldn't like to end up in a Community Home, like other crooks of your age who get caught, would you? This isn't just a run to throw them off the scent, like last time you went, this is the real thing.'

Colin said nothing for a few minutes, gazing out to sea in case he could spot the *Cornish Princess*. 'You mean, tonight you're really smuggling things in,' he said as a statement of fact. The outboard motor if nothing else convinced him.

'Not me—*we*,' corrected the other, 'both of us.'

'Where does it all go?'

'Since we're now partners, I'll tell you. When we bring the stuff in, we dump it—near the beach, in the village, all sorts of places. Then it's collected from there, that night or the next day, and taken to outlying farms all around, and there it stays for a year. It stays for a year while the heat dies down. Then after a year it goes on the market—oh, anywhere. Birmingham, f'instance. So now you know. And you've got to keep your mouth shut for certain, because if you don't, we're all going to say you took willing part in it. Because now you're going to.'

The *Cornish Princess* appeared before them, and they joined it. The same two men Colin had encountered previously were on board. Colin heard Derek ask the man at the wheel, who was still smoking a pipe as if it was attached to him, if his Dad had fixed the other thing, and he was answered with a nod of the head and a grunt. The other thing, whatever it was, could not mean anything to do with him, and Colin fell to wondering what Derek had been enquiring about. Whatever it was, Mr Trewan was involved, and Colin now saw how the operation worked.

The boys of the village were organized by Derek on behalf of his father, to act as a decoy to draw others from the scent, and from what Derek had instructed the boys earlier, not even most of their parents knew what was taking place. He would bet that most of the parents regarded the whole thing as innocent amusement. However, the boys themselves knew, that was certain. It would start as a risky but exciting game in an area where there was not much other excitement to stimulate them—but once they had taken part, they were too frightened to get out of it.

Darkness was now around them, thick and black within another hour, and the only sounds were the chug of the engine and the occasional swish of water from under the hull, and sometimes a liquid sucking sound from the helmsman's pipe. Even the second man on board was silent, and when he saw that Colin was cold from the breeze over the sea he handed him a sweater, blue like his own, without a word. It was too large, but it was warm, especially when Colin snuggled down on a seat underneath the forward canopy of the boat well out of the wind. Derek remained standing, leaning near the little array of darkened dials and staring forward into the night.

Then: 'Any time now,' said the helmsman, glancing at his watch by the light of a dim torch, and flicked a switch to put on the navigation lights. Not far in the distance similar lights appeared, as if they had been waiting for the signal, and the two sets of lights approached each other. The man who had lent Colin the sweater picked up a larger torch from somewhere below and flashed it three times in the direction of the other craft, then after a pause flashed three times again. Answering flashes came back through the night. Then the two boats were alongside each other, and the engines were switched off, and ropes passed between the two to secure them together.

For the moment, Colin could not see why a different method was being used from the time when he had hidden on board the dinghy, but he soon found out.

'Come on, Ginger,' ordered Derek, 'you're going to help in this. There's a very big load.'

The second boat was much larger, and seemed to be some kind of fishing boat. Colin could count four men on board, humping barrels on to the deck from below and stacking them at the side nearest to the *Cornish Princess*. Reluctantly Colin joined Derek at the gunwale. Two of the men from the other boat would raise a barrel and pass it to himself and Derek, who would take it between them and lower it into their own boat. Further along the boat, the helmsman and his mate were doing the same. The operation took place in total silence, and the crew of the other boat, whom Colin took to be Frenchmen, worked swiftly as if in a great hurry.

Within minutes the edges of the deck of the *Cornish Princess* were hidden under barrels, standing side by side on their ends for the sake of stability, then another row was laid down. He was panting a little by the time the last had been passed over, not so much with the weight which he had been lifting but with the speed at which they had all worked. Then a short, dapper man jumped lightly across from the other boat and a mumbled conversation took place between him and the helmsman, and while he could catch only an odd word here and there he was sure that the language used was part French and part English. The helmsman walked heavily across and down the steps to where the lavatory was, and immediately came on deck again carrying a small parcel in brown paper. The Frenchman brought a small torch out of his pocket and inspected the contents.

Colin, with his mind on drugs as another possibility, stepped forward cautiously to see. The parcel contained bundles of ten-pound notes, packed flat. The Frenchman clicked off the torch and skipped back on board his own boat, aided by one of his crew.

Then there was another pause, and Colin was impatient to be off. If he arrived in the village very late, his mother and Aunt Daphne might both start asking questions to which he would be able to give no answer. Four more figures appeared on the deck of the other boat, and at first he thought they were more members of the crew, but even in the vague illumination given out by the navigation lights he could see that somehow they were of a different shape. As the last of the four stood on board the deck of the Cornish craft, the ropes were cast off, both engines roared a little, and the boats drew apart.

'Come on, you,' said the man who had lent him his spare sweater, and pushed the four figures down the steps to the lavatory. As the last entered the small space outside the lavatory door, he switched on a light and Colin could now see clearly. Four men, three young and one old, with dark skins, stood apprehensively at the bottom of the steps. 'Now you stay down here, and I'm going to put the light out—right?'

He switched the light off again, came up and closed the door behind him.

So that was the meaning of tonight being the big night! The navigation lights were extinguished once more and the boat headed for home. Colin returned to his seat, and this time Derek joined him with a satisfied air.

'I don't think much of your business,' said Colin bitterly.

'Then mind yours,' retorted Derek briefly. 'If they're fool enough to pay, let 'em.'

'But they're illegal immigrants!'

'So what? Do you know how much they pay to come here?—more than twelve hundred pounds! And do you know what our cut is?—four hundred apiece. That's sixteen hundred pounds just for giving them transport.'

'What happens to them then?' demanded Colin.

'Your friend worrying about a cargo of trash?' grunted the helmsman, speaking with his pipe clenched firmly between his teeth. 'Once they're ashore, who cares what happens to them? That's their affair. Our job's done when we've landed them and got them far enough away from the harbour that they won't recognize it—or us—again.'

Colin shut up, but wondered how these Indians had been persuaded to pay over money for a venture which could so easily end in disaster for them. If they were caught, they would be deported, and whatever happened they would never see any of their cash again. And to raise such huge sums of money they had probably put themselves into debt for years to come. The next thing that he wondered was where the immigrants were to be put ashore, whether at Geraint's Cove or on a beach near St Ives. He recalled how Mr Mitchell had suddenly become excited when he had heard that Mr Trewan had been in St Ives talking to a boatman.

Ahead he could just vaguely make out the lights in Geraint's Cove when he heard a noise of engines from not far away. The man at the wheel had clearly heard the same sound, for he switched off the engine of the *Cornish Princess* abruptly, and knocked out his pipe on the heel of his boot. They all stayed motionless, and the boat rocked on the swell. Colin felt like calling out, but knew that if he did the others would implicate him in what was taking place, beyond any doubt at all. Navigation lights came on about a hundred yards away, then a strong searchlight swept across the water until it found them, and then a second searchlight stabbed through the night with precision and the two held them in their cold, hard stare.

From across the water as the other boat moved in quickly he could just hear the words: 'Stand by for boarding.' The two men and Derek sat down, the man with the pipe with his hand over his eyes as his head bent forward, like a man thinking.

It was just as there was a bump as the other boat touched them that Derek leapt to his feet and ran to the stern of the boat, dived overboard and began swimming, in a movement which took Colin by complete surprise. Then the *Cornish Princess* had five newcomers on board, four of them in uniform and two of them armed with guns which they had taken out of white holsters at their waists. The fifth was wearing a raincoat, and he stepped on board last, picking his way over the barrels on the deck.

'Good evening,' he said politely to Colin. 'Have we anything or anybody down below?' And he kicked open the door at the forward end of the wheelhouse. It was Mr Mitchell.

'Derek's gone overboard,' stated Colin dully to one of the armed men, the one known as Blake.

'Hope he can swim, then,' said the man, putting his gun away. 'Man in the water,' he called back to his own ship. One of the searchlights swung round and in its light Colin soon saw the head of Derek as he crawl-stroked towards the shore as fast as he was able. A dinghy was lowered and set out after him. 'Bit young for this game, aren't you?' resumed the man in a not very friendly tone.

'You can leave him alone,' said Mr Mitchell, coming back on deck with the four Indians in front of him. 'You might say that he's one of our best men,' he added, looking round first to ensure that the two crewmen of the boat had been taken on board the cutter and so would not be able to overhear.

Mr Blake smiled at Colin. 'Well, if he's with you, Sir, that's different. Now, gentlemen, kindly step on board the other boat.' The four foreigners obeyed despondently, and Colin felt sorry for them.

'One armed guard for this boat,' instructed Mr Mitchell to the cutter, 'if you please.'

'Right you are, Sir. Blake, remain on board.'

They cast off, and as soon as the engine had been re-started on the *Cornish Princess*, the cutter drew away at great speed, leaving a wake which could be seen even in the darkness. The searchlights were extinguished one after the other. Mr Mitchell was at the wheel, but he made no effort to set the boat in motion.

'When I was younger,' he said conversationally, 'my ambition was to drive a railway engine. We haven't got one of those with us, but I wonder if you have any ambition towards driving a boat? Just head towards those lights in the distance, will you, while we search the boat?'

Colin jumped at the chance, and after a minute's guidance the two others on board left him to it.

'And now,' said Mr Mitchell, when he and the other man had rescued Colin from the problems of getting the boat into the harbour and the craft was safely moored, 'we'd better see about getting you home.'

'But you'll never catch those on shore who were going to collect the barrels,' said Colin, who had just begun to worry about it.

'Oh yes we shall,' said Mr Mitchell. 'We've had the police hiding there for the past hour. Tonight's been a big night for all of us, hasn't it?'

FIFTEEN

BREAKING THE SPELL

The beach café did not open the next day, much to the annoyance of the holidaymakers in the cove, as Colin discovered when he went there in the afternoon. He knew it wouldn't. Mr Trewan was no longer in the village but had been in custody since early that morning. So was Derek. Mark had left the village to stay with relatives somewhere, because his parents had sent him. But the rest of the village appeared normal, in fact it possessed a normality which had not been visible since Colin and his mother had arrived there, somehow, for there were boys in the streets who seemed extra-cheerful, and when Colin ventured out he was greeted by all of those whom he encountered like a long-lost friend and treated in the village shop. Together they all went down to the beach and played games in and out of the visitors for an hour or two, adding to the visitors' annoyance.

And as the afternoon passed, and the tide began to come in, they all repaired to the pool as if drawn to examine some former wild animal which was now dead and so was safe to approach.

'It's like a bathing pool,' said some man who had followed on behind to discover if there was some interesting sight these local boys knew about.

'We know,' said Colin, standing at the edge of the amphitheatre with the rest of the boys and inspecting its surface. The level of the water had risen until it was high enough up the table rock.

'You could swim in that,' resumed the man. 'Is it warm?'

Nobody answered him. Fred was standing alongside Colin and looked at him, and Colin could see that all the village boys were waiting for some sort of sign. He was not absolutely certain what they wanted, but it was rather as if in the adult world a banquet were being held and the rest could not sit until the guest of honour was seated. Nobody moved, and a little crowd of visitors gathered behind to find out what they were missing.

Colin looked at Fred, and Fred smiled in a sort of encouragement. 'I'm glad we don't have to any more,' remarked Fred casually.

That settled it. Colin could see what was missing and what had to be done to break the final hold of Derek over the village, and he didn't hesitate. He sauntered over towards the black rocks and just as casually began to ascend, and the boys as at a signal climbed up after him, seating themselves to watch and wait. Colin reached the pinnacle and the sun shining on his mop of hair made it glow more of a golden colour, and in the curious light up there with the beams coming obliquely so that half of him was in shadow he almost looked tanned.

Then he lowered himself on to the ledge and stood facing the water and the gathering of visitors which had now swelled to perhaps fifty. Fred squatted on the pinnacle behind him, and down below Colin could see the figure of Simon, still with his arm in a sling of course, seated down by the bottom end of the pool. There was complete silence. Even the holiday-makers could sense that something of importance was about to happen.

He looked down carefully, judged the distance, and dived. As he returned to the air the entire surface broke up as boys dived in from all sides, until the pool was full of swimming boys, and he heard as in the distance a faint ripple of hands clapping as the applause of the visitors died away. The show was over, and with the spell broken the people moved away.

'Got to see to the cows now,' said Fred, coming up to him very soon afterwards. 'Do you want to come to the youth club tonight? Seven o'clock at the church hall?'

'Call for me,' said Colin. 'Wait a bit, I'll walk back to the village with you.'

When they left, the others were still in the pool, splashing around happily. A green van was parked outside Aunt Daphne's when he got there.

'We've been waiting for you,' said his mother. The best tea things were out on the table. 'Where have you been?'

'Oh, leave the boy alone, Mary,' said Mr Mitchell.

Mary? Colin's ears pricked up uncertainly. When he had been deposited at the door of the cottage the previous night Mr Mitchell had driven away immediately, with a verbal message for Colin to give his mother that he would be round some time the following day to explain his late arrival home that night. He had not given his mother the message, partly because she had been cross at the lateness of the hour and not inclined to hear explanations, and partly because the explanation had been too involved at a time when he had been unable to think straight.

'Your mother and I know each other,' said Mr Mitchell without preamble. 'Up to last year, we both worked in the same offices in Birmingham.'

So that was it! He knew that his mother was a secretary in the Customs and Excise offices in the city centre, but only now did it all fit together.

'And then he got moved to Cornwall,' put in Aunt Daphne, 'where he's spent some time investigating us. Now come and have your tea. When you've washed your hands,' she added.

'When Aunt Daphne mentioned Mr Mitchell,' said his mother, 'it just didn't click, especially when he was supposed to be an artist.'

'I was a little worried in the church last Sunday,' explained George Mitchell when Colin returned from the kitchen, 'in case your mother recognized me. I wasn't sure whether I ought to get up and leave at once, or stay put and hope she didn't see me. I decided to sit still—you know, like an animal does when it's camouflaged. It's movement that makes people see you. And she didn't see me and so I could slip away quietly at the end.'

'Well now,' said Aunt Daphne, firmly cutting short further unnecessary pleasantries and making herself more comfortable in her chair at the far end of the table from Colin, 'I have been working a few things out while everyone has been chatting this afternoon, and I have decided to expand further into the holiday business. The first thing to think about is that beach café, which now looks like being empty for a long time.'

She cleared her throat. 'Mary, give George some more tea. Yes. Now, you can't have a holiday beach like ours without providing refreshment. It's not fair to the tourists. It'll have to stay closed for the rest of this season, I've no doubt, but after that—well, I've decided that I shall open it again.'

Colin looked up with interest. He could not imagine this elderly lady serving behind the counter in that or any other café. 'But what if Mr Trewan won't sell it to you?' he said.

'Why, Trewan doesn't own it, he only rents it. He won't buy anything if he can avoid it. Charlie Smith owns the premises. And he,' she said slowly with some kind of meaning which was not apparent to the rest of them yet, 'was telling me only this February that he wanted to be shot of it. I think Charlie would sell it at a very reasonable price if I wanted to buy it. He certainly would,' she added as if she had suddenly noticed a blot on Charlie Smith's exercise book and would accept no excuse.

'Now with that café goes the house just behind it. Of course, it's only a seasonal sort of business, but our season down here stretches from April to late September, and I know the profits are very good indeed. It could be a bargain. I shall purchase the whole thing.'

Colin's mother said something to the effect that her aunt would not be able to keep an eye on the business properly even if she did buy it, and Colin himself was reminded irresistibly of when he had played the game of Monopoly at a friend's house. Buy the property and put a house on it. What came next did not appear in the Monopoly rules, how ever.

'I don't intend to keep an eye on it, Mary,' she said. 'What do you take me for, at my age? I've got more than enough with the holiday cottage, thank you. No, I'm going to sell it to you.'

Colin's mother said faintly that she couldn't possibly afford it, but her objection was brushed aside with a 'Nonsense— how much mortgage do you pay on that house of yours in Birmingham? Sell it. Use the money from that to stock up the café, and from the profits you can pay me back, like paying a mortgage. Besides, it's healthier air for Colin round here—you can see how he's getting roses in his cheeks already! After all, if I can't help the only relatives I've got left, who else can I help? Leave my money to a home for stray cats? I should think so!'

The boy's heart gave a sudden leap, and he looked anxiously towards his mother, while she in turn looked anxiously to wards George Mitchell. The latter put down his cup and screwed up his face a little while he thought. 'Living on the premises, so no travel to get to work. That cuts expenses. No competition whatever for the hundreds of customers who go down to that beach every day during the season—have you ever seen the queues of people waiting to get inside that café?'

She shook her head, without saying a word, and Colin's hopes rose further.

'The profits must be considerable. I reckon that in the summer you'd make twice as much money each month, even with an assistant, as you get working in the office, so if in the winter you sell nothing at all you're still no worse off, taking the year as a whole. Pleasant climate, house provided, no worries.'

He paused. 'I don't see how you could possibly lose.'

'Then that,' said Aunt Daphne, 'is settled. All I shall have to do is have a good talk with Charlie Smith, and then see my solicitor to make it all legal. When do you plan to start?'

'You mean it?' cried Colin.

'Of course I mean it. So when you leave here, in a few weeks' time, the next time you come it will be to live here. You just give me until tomorrow night to arrange it properly. When you go back to your studio, George, call in at Charlie Smith's, if you'll be so kind. He lives in the third house down the hill towards the harbour. It's much too big for him. Tell him I would like to see him tomorrow morning, about ten.'

'He might not come, Aunt Daphne,' said Colin quietly. 'What then?'

'I don't think you need worry about that,' said Aunt Daphne, and she meant it.

When George Mitchell finally left, Colin and his mother saw him to door, and then Colin waited until he was about to get into the little green van.

'What—' he began, then stopped. It was important, and he wanted to get the words right, but it was no use, he could not think of any better way to ask what he wanted to know. 'What will happen to Fred, and the others in the village?'

Mr Mitchell looked him straight in the face as he said: 'Why, what should happen to them?'

'Well, I mean, the smuggling and all that.'

'I would say,' said Mr Mitchell, 'that it would be very difficult indeed trying to prove anything against them, so why waste time and money in trying?'

'And what about Fred's uncle, at the farm?'

'Oh yes, I did receive information one evening lately that he has in his possession a barrel which is believed to contain smuggled goods. Now I have reason to believe that the barrel is hidden in a barn.' He sounded very official and cold, like a policeman doing his duty. 'Well, tomorrow afternoon I shall have to investigate that barn, and if I find the barrel there I shall have to take appropriate action. Of course, if by any accident anyone tips him off—say tomorrow morning—and I can't find any such barrel—in his barn— then obviously the information would have been inaccurate.'

Colin said that it might be wrong for anyone to give a tip-off to Fred's uncle, just in case he hadn't understood correctly what Mr Mitchell was getting at.

'I think,' said George Mitchell, 'that right or wrong, if any boy living in this village knew what I was going to do he'd certainly do what he could to protect another resident, especially if he knew that the smuggling had ended for good. After all, it's been a Cornish pastime for centuries. And I'm a Cornishman, too, don't forget.'

Colin smiled happily.

'That's why I know nothing about a fogou, either. Now tell your mother,' said Mr Mitchell, 'that when you've settled in, I shall probably be seeing a lot of her—if you approve, of course.'

Colin did approve, and turned a cartwheel before he entered the house. In ten minutes, Fred would be round so they could go to the youth club.